Malcolm Havard

Malcolm Havard writes both fiction and non-fiction.

He has written five non-fiction books, ghost written three others and has published four novels and a collection of short stories.

Born near Sheffield he was educated at the Universities of Sheffield and Aberdeen and now lives in Cheshire.

Also by Malcolm Havard

The Last Mountain
Contrail
Touched
The First Book of Gabriel
Hurricane Season

L.M.F.

First Published worldwide in 2019

The right of Malcolm Havard to be identified as the Author
of the Work has been asserted by him in accordance
with the Copyright, Design and Patents Act 1988

Malcolm Havard

During WW2, RAF Bomber Command crews suffered an extremely high casualty rate: 55,573 killed out of a total of 125,000 aircrew (a 44.4 percent death rate) during one of the most contentious and controversial campaigns of the whole conflict.

This book does not comment on the morality or correctness of the RAF's activities but concentrates on the experience of one crew on one night and, by design, contains 55,573 words.

LMF - PROLOGUE

27/1/44 1.51 am

J ust drop the bastard bombs, Saunders.'

The anger had gone out of Taylor's voice. Even over the intercom, Roland could hear the shock and anguish. The vision was clearly getting to him too. But then, it was more than just what he saw, all of his senses were experiencing the burning city. It would be the same for the rest of the crew as well.

His face was uncomfortably warm like he was sat too close to the hearth at home. The heat radiated through the Perspex, the metal skin of the aircraft was hot to the touch. Even over the roar of the engines, the rush of air, the vibrations, he could hear the crackle of the fire and the crash as buildings collapsed. C-Charlie bumped and tossed in the superheated air. The stench was awful, smoke, chemicals; the smell of burned meat told its own story of what things were like beneath.

But there was one thing that was worse than that: he could taste it. Burnt human flesh and the fabric and content of their destroyed homes sat on his tongue. As he swallowed, he took it down inside him. It was like he was eating the city.

'Drop them, just drop the bastards! Please!'

INVESTIGATION
1

Murray stood awkwardly in front of the Squadron Leader's desk, awaking long buried memories of being called to the Headmaster over some indiscretion.

His discomfort was odd. He was at least a decade older than the man he stood in front of and they held the same rank. But the nature of Bomber Command meant the combat experience of the 24-year-old, a grizzled veteran of some 60 missions over enemy territory, meant he was de facto superior.

And he knew it.

He was clearly irritated. 'For God's sake, what the hell does Group want? I thought I'd been put in charge to get results and run things as I see fit. Surely that applies to discipline, they know that don't they?'

'Well, yes, of course.'

'So what's all this about? This is questioning my authority.' He jabbed his finger at the file.

The file that had been thrust at Murray by his section head the previous afternoon.

'Take a look at this,' he'd been told. 'Looks like it's in

your remit. See what you think.'

That was it, the sum of his instructions. That and the travel warrant to the Fen country. That clearly said; 'go and find out' clearer than any orders.

So here he was.He kept calm, knowing that diplomacy was the key

'Harvey, I'm sure it's not, it'll be someone high up getting the wind up for some reason. I'm sure it's nothing. I've just been asked to take another look, that's all.'

He felt a little sick and extremely uneasy, he'd had to force himself not to use Harvey's rank as a title, to gently remind the man that their ranks, if not experience were equal. It was a line in the sand he had to draw.

'Well it's bloody ridiculous if you ask me. Psychological mumbo-jumbo, junk ideas of how things should be done made up by people who've never even flown over Germany.'

Murray felt himself redden. Harvey had landed a blow where he was most vulnerable.

'I'm sure you're right, Squadron Leader,' he said, then kicked himself for weakening. 'Look, it's what I've been ordered to do. I honestly don't know why, maybe he's got friends in High Places, who knows? All I know is that I've been asked to have a look at the files and see if I can work out what happened.'

'It's patently obvious what happened.'

Murray took a deep breath. 'I know. It must be bloody annoying. I know you have a squadron to run and…'

'Yes, I have. I've no time for this. There are more than 400 people on the base who I'm responsible for, why should I care about this one?'

On cue, only slightly muffled by the window panes which rattled with the vibration, an engine coughed, caught and then roared into life. The sound was unmistakable, rich, deep, mellow yet savage, a Rolls Royce Merlin, a ground test breaking the chill stiffness of the Winter's morning. Somehow it stiffened Murray's resolve.

'Seven,' he said.

'What do you mean seven?'

'There are seven in the crew.'

Harvey shrugged. 'So? You don't think I know that?'

'Of course I do. It's just that only one of them was disciplined...'

'So?' said Harvey again.

Patience.

'They were all on the mission. Group is concerned about morale, things like this can affect it badly. Those seven will have pals -'

'Six of them do,' said Harvey.

'Six then. Those six will talk to their pals and they, in turn, will talk. What happened to them will ripple through the rest of the crews, then the ground crew and the WAAFs and -'

'Gossip, nothing more. I'd rather have that spread than malingering and cowardice. That needs to be nipped in the bud.'

'Yes, of course it does but -'

'Look, Murray, what are you looking to prove? What's your agenda?'

Murray paused. Interesting, Harvey was being more than defensive, he was aggressively so. Perhaps there was something in this after all? For the first time he really wanted to look at the files.

'I don't have an agenda, I promise. It's just something that's come down from the medics. Look, I'm sure you're right and everything has been done properly. I'm just another pair of eyes looking things over, it's just a paper exercise, it needn't be too disruptive. Just put me in an office somewhere with the files, I'll give them a quick shufty and then I'll be gone and out of your hair.'

He waited whilst Harvey chewed the stem of his unlit pipe, a frown on his young, lined face.

'Oh, for God's sake, all right,' he said at last. 'If you must. Let's get this farce over with. Harrison! Harrison, get in here!' He looked up at Murray and, almost as an afterthought, smiled at him. 'Sorry, old boy,' he added in a softer tone. 'Got a lot on my plate. I know this isn't your fault. I'll get Harrison here,' he nodded at the corporal who had stepped into the office. 'To sort out the paperwork on the case and find you somewhere to work.'

Murray forced himself not to sigh in relief.

'Thank you,' he said.

'Then, when you're done, we can have a spot of lunch. If you're not hurrying off, of course.'

The line was delivered casually but the message was crystal clear. Lunch was at 12.30 sharp on bases like this. Harvey wanted everything over and nicely swept under the carpet in just over two hours.

Murray forced himself to smile.

'Of course, that would be nice,' he said

*

10.36 am, 6th February 1944

Murray stood the cold for ten minutes before deciding comfort trumped service protocol and donned his overcoat and scarf.

The office he'd been given had a table and a window but no radiator or stove and was, effectively, little more than a

13

glorified storeroom. It did, at least, have a view across the airfield to the hangars.

It was a dank, cold, miserably grey morning. He could see the mechanics working on the black giants and doubted that they were any colder than him, even though they were outside. At least they had the chance to move around whilst he was forced into inaction by the task. All that faced him was the prospect of getting ever colder.

He really should start, he knew that, but he could not help staring at the machines and think where they would be tonight, if the fog did not close in and scrub the mission of course. Handley-Page Halifaxes, not the best that Bomber Command had, not the Lancasters that could seemingly do everything, but good enough. During the day they would be checked over, the basic servicing would be done, urgent repairs undertaken, then they would be loaded with fuel and bombs, high explosive and/or incendiaries, and the crew would board them. They would lumber down the runway, one by one, waddle into the air taking their deadly cargo and their young, fragile, frightened crew on a trip of several hours over hostile territory filled with dangers - flak, night fighters, collisions and mechanical failures - in a stream of five, six or seven hundred others.

The war was being won but no-one seemed to have told the Germans because the cost was rising. The losses were becoming alarming, 5% became 7%, then 8, 9 and 10%. Where would it stop? He knew the numbers only too well; even at 5% statistically no crew would survive 25 mission. At 10% loss rates, they'd only reach ten.

A tour was 30 missions long.

The men knew these numbers. It took a special kind of courage to head off, night after night, knowing those odds. They were not stupid, they saw their friends disappear, the familiar faces in the mess would be replaced by fresh-faced newcomers. Yet still they got into their machines and took off, willingly facing the dangers and the statistical certainty of fate to try to hit the target and then get home again.

At least most of them did.

Which brought him back to the files arranged on the table in front of him. Eight files, seven personnel files and a Court of Inquiry report, the latter dealing with the events of the mission a week or so before.

He had lined up the personnel files on the left side of the desk, the inquiry report in the centre and his notepad to the right. As he looked down the row of personnel files, he noticed that he had, unconsciously, arranged them in the order that they would have sat in their Halifax from front to back:

Pilot-Officer Arthur Terrence Howard - Bomb Aimer

Flying-Officer Roland Saunders - Navigator
Flight-Sergeant Douglas Atkinson-Greive - Pilot
Flight-Sergeant Albert Harrison - Flight Engineer
Flight-Sergeant John Hiley - Radio Operator
Flying-Officer Gerald Pascoe - Mid-upper Gunner
Flying-Officer Adam Taylor - Rear Gunner

All of the files were essentially the same, shaded with the buff hue of bureaucracy. Except one. He tried to ignore the letter stamped on the front, but it was large, bold and red and impossible to miss.

A red W. For Waverer.

But it meant LMF.

Lack of Moral Fibre. A brand of shame, the ultimate damning character judgement made by the Royal Air Force on one of its members.

He picked up the Court of Inquiry report and started to read.

LMF 1

'The pilot, Sergeant Douglas Atkinson-Grieve, reported some difficulty sleeping in the night before the mission. This is not believed to be significant or indicative of an underlying medical problem.'

Extract from the Medical Officer's note to the Court of Inquiry

26/1/44 4.50am

The sensational symphony of being awake in the small hours of the morning were gratingly familiar. The squeaks and squawks from the institutional metal-framed bed as it bore his weight, the rasp of the rough wool blanket on his skin as it balled and twisted into uncomfortable knots, the background must of male odours, stale tobacco and yesterday's cabbage passed through young guts, the heavy breathing and sighing of his roommate drifting in and out of sleep.

Whilst he wanted the oblivion of sleep, he dreaded the nerve-jangling journey his mind conducted him on, dreams half-remembered or vividly clear, leaving him sweat-soaked and shaken.

But now he was awake and what he needed right now was a cigarette and a piss. He couldn't think of anything else.

No. That was not true.

One thing was always on his mind.

One thing that was really many things, many sensations, myriad thrills and nameless, innumerable fears. It was terrifying, sickening but was heart-thumpingly thrilling, raw and vital, filling him, consumed him, frightened yet completed him. It was something he did not want to do but could not do without.

Like getting up and having a cigarette and a piss, in that order.

He kicked the blanket away, relinquishing the warmth, and landed in the darkness fumbling for his Players and matches. His fingers were trembling, clumsy, he dropped the first cigarette, spilled half the matches but, finally, managed to hold onto one of each. The familiarity of the strike was comforting, the roughness of the sandpaper, splintered sparks, sulphurous fumes, the flare, harsh on the eyes and searing on fingertips, the subtle change in the flame as chemicals burning turned to the consumption of the wood.

'What the fuck?' grunted his roommate. 'It's five in the bleedin' morning.'

Douglas ignored him. He lit his cigarette and drew the smoke inside him. Only then did he reply.

'So?' he said.

'What do you mean, so? I'm trying to bloody well sleep!'

But the words were already behind him. He had slipped unstockinged feet into stiff, cold shoes, grabbed his sweater from his chair and coat from the hook on the door and was clomping down the corridor to the toilets. Inside was the sour bite of urine, weak beer and disinfectant, his breath fogged and mingled with the steam from the liquid held hot within him. He was impatient to finish, even before he had he was pulling the sweater over his head and slipping his arms through the sleeves of his coat, even so he remembered to splash water on his hands. Habits reinforced with the aid of a ruler could not be forgotten.

He walked out into the night, a night that was morning. Douglas raised his head, felt the breeze on his cheeks. It was bitter, easterly, gusting but the sky was full of stars, the snow-flecked ground hard.

He smiled. Yes! Today, tonight, it would happen.

He knew that all around him, hidden in the gloom were giants, black, shrouded, patiently waiting. He did not look for them, instead he headed for the hulking mass of the nearest hangar, found the door, opened it and stepped quickly inside.

'Oy! Watch that bloody light - oh, beg your pardon, sir.'

He let them believe he was an officer, why not? 'Carry on, sergeant,' he said.

He didn't stop to chat, he had eyes for only one thing.

The machine. It was pristine, paint barely dry, markings fresh, undented, unscarred, straight from the factory, Merlin engines barely run in, its guns unfired.

A virgin.

But a weapon of war.

A Halifax.

LMF 2

'SAUNDERS is a navigator who had served in ATKINSON-GRIEVE's original crew. He had just returned to the squadron after recovering from a non-operational injury. Prior to his injury. SAUNDERS had completed 14 missions.'

Court of Inquiry report extract.

26/1/44 6 am

Someone had left the light on on the landing. A narrow shaft of light from the door was projected diagonally across the bed, terminating on the pillow where it bathed a mass of golden curls in its soft, yellowish glow.

She had rolled away from him sometime in the night, a natural yet symbolic act. He had been able to get up without disturbing her and he'd now been sat by the bed for twenty minutes just watching and waiting.

She was beautiful, he'd always thought so even when it had not been right to say so. One of her shoulders had escaped from the sheets, a perfect, graceful globe, alabaster white, flawless. He wanted so much to kiss it, to press his lips against her skin, against the neck and the top of her spine visible beneath the golden halo and the bedclothes.

He wanted to but couldn't, his desire ill-timed and his guilt greater now than it had been the previous evening.

He closed his eyes and sighed, perhaps not as quietly as he intended for the light clicked on. He opened them and found he was staring into hers. She squinted at him, she had rolled over and half raised herself from the bed revealing more of the voluptuous promise that lay beneath the sheets.

Then he saw her eyes focus on his uniform and she slumped back down again with a sigh of her own and buried her face in the pillow.

'It can't be that time already.'

Her muffled words were a statement of resignation not a question.

'It's after six,' he said. 'My leave ends at eight.'

She did not reply. He waited a few more seconds then rose , retrieved his shoes from beneath the bed, sat again and started to put them on. As he tied the laces, he asked the question he guessed both had been dreading.

'Will you be alright getting back on your own?'

'I'm going to have to be, aren't I?'

The tartness of her reply stung.

'I've paid the bill. You should get breakfast.'

'Oh yes, that will be nice. I'll enjoy having everyone looking at me.'

'But...'

'Oh yes, everyone will believe that I'm really Mrs Saunders, I know, of course they will.'

He stared at her for a few moments in the desperate hope that words of solace would come come but knowing that they wouldn't.

'I'll see you later,' he said.

He got up and walked across the room, intent on getting his coat but did not reach it for, in a flurry of bedclothes, she was with him, her nakedness pressed against him, soft, sleek, firm, cream against blue and silver. They stood in eloquent silence until the warmth of the night left her body and she began to shake.

'You're cold,' he said. 'Get back into bed. I've got…'

'You've got to go, I know.'

Still, he had to push her away to reach for his coat and, when he did, the sharp stab of pain from his shoulder made him gasp.

'It's not right,' she said, helping pull the sleeve onto his arm. 'You're not fit. Surely they can't make you fly like this.'

'The medics say I am, and, after all, I'm fit enough to use a slide rule and read a map.' He fastened the buttons of his coat with his good hand. 'Connie,' he said quietly. 'We…'

She silenced him with a kiss.

'I know,' she said afterwards. 'But I still need a little time.'

LMF 3

'Radio operator - Sergeant HILEY (dob 22/12/1925, 0 missions)'

26/1/44 7 am

J ohn was up before his alarm went off, partly because he was already awake but mostly because he was afraid of his new roommate.

He hadn't expected the coldness of his reception. He'd arrived on the evening train and reported to the squadron office. They'd checked his orders and allocated his room. It had been empty when he'd arrived, so he had unpacked in silence, putting his belongings in his locker and hanging his uniforms and shirt in the utilitarian wardrobe. He then sat on the bed and looked at the other side of the room, wondering who he was sharing with.

There were a few clues to their identity from the photographs by the bed. There were two, in simple, cheap frames. One was of a woman, matronly, straggly hair up in a loose bun. She was stood on a verandah, posing awkwardly like she had something that needed to be done urgently and didn't have the time to wait. The house was wooden, with a corrugated tin roof, and obviously not in England. The other photograph was of children, four of them, two girls and two boys ranging in ages from perhaps 5 or 6 to 14 or 15, dressed in their Sunday best, a posed, studio portrait.

His roommate's mother and siblings? That seemed to be the most likely. Where was he from? South Africa? Possibly but more likely Australian, yes, that would be it.

He wondered what it would be like to have so many brothers and sisters or, indeed, any at all. He looked at his own photograph, also placed by the bed on the bedside table, his father bald with his small, metal-framed glasses, his mother grey haired, thin and tall. It had always been just the three of them.

His musings on this had been interrupted by his room-mate's arrival. He had got to his feet, held out his hand.

'Oh, hello,' he had said. 'I'm John. John Hiley and I've -'

'Strewth! Fuck me, that's all I bloody well need,' the man had muttered and, ignoring John's hand, laid down on the other bed.

He had lain with his his hands behind his head, staring at the ceiling and not said another word. He had brought a stench with him, sweat, stale beer and cigarette smoke which John found highly unpleasant, but which he was not going to say anything about. John picked up his book and laid down himself, though he did not really read. What had he done to get that reaction?

He wondered what situation he'd landed in. The man was much older than he'd expected, though how old he wasn't sure. Forty, fifty? And what had happened to his face? It was scarred, crisscrossed with fine lines. Had he been in a fight, an accident? The woman must be his wife, John supposed, and the children his.

They had not exchanged another word when, without asking, his roommate had got up, undressed and turned the light out. He did, however, say something when John had set up his travel alarm.

'If that fucking thing's tickin' keeps me awake I'll ram it up your fucking arse,' he'd grunted, at which point he'd rolled over and started snoring, leaving John laid petrified in the dark.

Now, in the morning, he carefully - and quietly -

turned the alarm off before it rang, picked up his uniform and wash things and gone off in search of the bathroom.

It was cold, spartan and no friendlier than his room, but no worse. He stared at his reflection in the mirror.

He'd always been alone, always the outsider; the only child, the scholarship boy in a school, miles from home, working as the only young clerk in his engineering company. Even at the HCU he'd ended up missing the important right-of-passage moment when the crews had come together because he'd had an operation on his ingrowing toenail.

Now he was on his own - again. A solitary posting to, what?

More miserable loneliness it seemed.

John did not really need to shave but he did anyway just to pass the time.

LMF 4

'Engineer - Sergeant HARRISON (dob 21/11/1907, 20 missions)'

26/1/44 7.10 am

Burt lay in the darkness for a few minutes after the kid had got up, then rolled out of bed, put the light on and lit a cigarette.

He stared at the other, empty bed. Christ, he looked young, he *was* young; Burt could have been the lad's father.

He looked across at the photo of his kids. Shane was tall in it then but that was taken over a year ago now, he'd be even bigger now. They were all growing up, he was missing that. He shouldn't have gone, shouldn't have answered the Old Country's call, he should have waited, gone to war against the Japs who were the real threat to the Aussie coast.

He shouldn't have but he had so there was no good moping about it. There was no changing things now.

But he knew that wasn't true. There was a reason, he just had to grasp the nettle.

He reached into the drawer of the nightstand and took out the letter. Mags didn't often write but her blocky, untidy script was unmistakable. He knew it off by heart but still read it again, skipping through the news about what was new in Bathurst, which was not very much, and what the children had been getting up to, which was considerable and reminded Burt of his own childhood. The more he read the letter, the more he realised that it had been rushed, that Mags had been distracted, her mind elsewhere. It was only in the last part where it became clear why she was like this and what the letter was about. There was even a small gap in the text, Burt could picture Mags stopping, thinking about what to say, taking a deep breath and starting.

'I have to go into the city next month. Doc Jackson wants me to have an op to cut out a lump he's been fussing about. The kids will be right, got my sister coming to stay. It aint nothing and I'll be back before anyone knows it.'

The words were benign but only on the surface - underneath they chilled him. The truth was Mags disliked her sister, in fact she hated her with a passion. The fact that she'd got her to come over spoke legions.

A lump. Cancer, it had to be even though she hadn't said it. Mags always feared it, it was in the family, her mother had it and died at 41, her aunt too. Mags would have pegged the washing out and done the baking even if she'd had her leg taken off, yet she was going to hospital, a place she was terrified of.

That said so much.

She was scared, in pain and on her own. And he was 12,000 miles away.

He should be with her, but he wasn't and why? He was here because he'd wanted to be here. He'd done what he'd wanted to do as he always had. He could have served at home, but the truth was he wanted the adventure. At what cost?

The cigarette had burned down, it was searing his fingers, yet he could not remember having smoked it. He stubbed it out and lit another, drawing the smoke deep into his lungs.

A lump. Cancer.

Mags had cancer.

He stared at her photo again, then at the one of the kids. The tears started to come.

He was on his feet in an instant, needing to do something to distract himself. There was water and bowl in the room, he'd shave here and think whilst he was doing it.

He stopped. The face that stared back from the mirror was old. He looked like his own father, flabby, grey, and very, very tired.

And there were the scars. He ran his fingers along them. The docs had done a good job in sewing him together, but they would always be there, jagged and white, a reminder.

Humpty-dumpty. The nursery rhyme came to him, unbidden. He'd sung it to all four of the kids, Mags had too, God knows why because it was so, twee, so...Pommy. He knew why he'd thought of it though, for him, he had been broken and put back together again, and for Mags.

Mags, cut open.

He nicked his cheek with the first stroke of the razor. Scarlet drops plopped into the water and stained it pink.

He almost threw up.

That decided it: he'd have to see the Old Man.

LMF 5

'Sergeant ATKINSON-GRIEVE is an experienced pilot who had completed 29 missions prior to the raid on ESSEN.'

26/1/44 7.33 am

Squadron Leader Harvey was reading the orders that had just come in from Group when he was interrupted by a knock on the door. He scowled. Everyone knew that he was not to be disturbed at this time. Irritated, he closed the file, ensuring that the target's identity was covered.

'Yes?' he called. 'What the devil is it?'

His office door opened. It was Heather, the WAAF whose duties doubled as his driver and secretary.

'Sorry to bother you, sir,' she said. 'But I've got Sergeant Atkinson-Grieve here and -'

'Dag? Of course you have, blast the man,' he said, not caring who heard. 'For God's sake, Heather, now? I'm up to my neck in it.'

'He's very insistent, sir.'

'He's a...' Harvey managed to stop saying what he wanted to call his pilot. 'Oh all right but make it quick.' He raised his voice for the last part, making it clear that he was addressing Dag.

The WAAF moved to one side and Dag stepped into the office. Harvey could see that he was excited, wide-eyed and positively bouncing on the balls of his feet.

'Sir, I've been down to the hangar and -'

'Where's your salute?' Harvey snapped. 'I'm your commanding officer!'

Dag looked startled for a moment, then snapped to attention. 'Sir, I -' he began.

'I didn't give you permission to speak, sergeant.'

Harvey saw Dag struggle to compose himself, which gave him some satisfaction. He let him stew for a few seconds but then realised that the biggest impact was on his own time.

'All right, what is it?' he said. 'Be quick.'

'Sir, I've been down to look at the new machine that's just arrived from the depot-'

'What of it?'

'Well, it's going to be ready for tonight and -'

'No,' said Harvey.

Dag was silent for a few moments.

'No, sir?' he said at last.

'No. I know what you're wanting and the answer's no.'

'But-'

'But nothing. You're not going to take the squadron's brand-new crate to finish your tour. I've other crews waiting for it, why should you get it before them?'

'Well, I've done 29 and as there's a mission tonight -'

'Who's said there is?' Harvey said but saw Dag's eyes go to the file on the desk. 'All right let's say for the moment there is. Just wait for the crew rosters to be posted. You might be needed as a spare.'

Harvey did not expect this to satisfy Dag, and he was right.

'But, sir, I've not flown for weeks. I've only done three

29

trips in the last two months. It's killing me, waiting.'

And why was that? Harvey had to bite his tongue not to say it. Why was it that no-one wanted to fly with Dag? He stared at his pilot and took a deep breath. Did every squadron have awkward types like Dag? He'd be glad to be shot of him.

And if he did one more, he would be. He'd have done a tour then, he could be posted out.

Harvey frowned. Perhaps this was an opportunity.

'Let's say you could get a crew,' he said.

'I can!' said Dag eagerly. 'There's plenty of spare bods around.'

'By 10 am, sharp,' said Harvey.

'Yes, sir, thank you, sir!' Dag started to leave.

'Wait!' said Harvey, sharply. 'You're still not having the new crate. The crew of C-Charlie are having that. You can have their old one.'

'C-Charlie? But sir, that's a dog. I'm the best-'

'Take it or leave it, Dag. You're not going to get anything else.'

Dag stared at him for a few seconds. 'I'll take it,' he muttered and turned to leave. Before Harvey could get the words out, he remembered to add, 'Sir,' and give a hasty salute.

'Ten sharp!' Harvey called at his retreating back.

LMF 6

'Sergeant ATKINSON-GRIEVE was informed that the squadron roster was complete but that an additional aircraft could be added to the roll if the pilot was able to assemble a crew from those not due to fly that night.'

26/1/44 7.43 am

Roland stopped his MG a little way short of the gatehouse but kept the engine running. It was still dark but, in the gloom, he was sure he could make out the hulking, black, four-engined giants sat quietly sleeping on their hardstandings, dispersed around the airfield. The vista was so familiar it was as if he was viewing it in bright daylight.

It was a vista he had not wished to see again.

He put the MG into gear and drove on before he had the chance to change his mind.

At the gate, the guard took his papers into his hut to read them and, as he handed them back, saluted and said, 'Welcome back, sir.'

Roland couldn't reply. He was in a daze, which continued as he drove up to the admin block. His heart was thumping, his mouth dry, he was light headed. He parked the car, got out, walked over to the entrance and was about to step inside when the door opened. He found himself face-to-face with the last person he wanted to see.

'Dag,' he said.

'Roly, just the man. I want a word with you.'

He took hold of Roland's arm and pulled him inside. It was obvious he was het up, excited. There could only be one reason for this.

'Dag,' he said. 'Look, I can explain -'

'Damn, Harvey's watching,' Dag muttered. 'Nosy bastard.' He straightened up, Roland waited for the punch but, to his surprise, Dag snapped to attention, saluted and said more loudly, 'Flying-Officer Saunders! Welcome back, sir.'

Roland saw Dag give a sly glance in the direction of the Squadron Leader's office.

'Er, thanks, Dag, but -'

'Let's walk.'

'But...I...I need to report to the office and...'

'That can wait. This is important. Come on.'

Dag lead him out into the darkness again then hustled him across the parade ground outside towards the maintenance hangars.

'Dag, what is it?' Roland said. 'Is this about Connie?'

Dag abruptly stopped. 'Connie?' he said. 'Why should it be? She's not here, she's on leave, some family emergency or something. Why, what have you heard? Is she all right?'

'Er, yes, as far as I know, I just thought...'

'You thought what?'

'Nothing. Forget it,' said Roland, quickly. 'So what's this about?'

'I need you,' Dag said.

'Need me? What for?'

Dag didn't immediately answer. Instead he grabbed hold of Roland and hurried him on. A few seconds later Roland realised where they were headed: towards a parked

Halifax.

Dag pointed up at it. 'For that? What else?'

Roland walked under the wing and looked up at the fuselage. He could just make out the squadron code and the letter C in the dull red paint.

'This is Mac's machine, isn't it?' he said.

'Not any more, it's ours.'

'Ours?' Then realisation hit him. 'You want me to crew with you, navigate?'

'Yes, of course, what else? You're fit now aren't you?'

'Well yes, but...'

'And you're a navigator.'

'Yes, of course, but...'

'Good. Well, you're in time for the briefings so we'll be fine. Now -'

'Wait,' said Roland. 'Briefings? You mean...the raid's today, tonight?'

'Yes, of course.'

'But...' Roland stopped and stared up at the Halifax again.

'But what? What's the problem?'

Roland knew exactly what the problem was; He was not ready to go back. He was scared. He wanted more time.

He wanted to say these things, but didn't, couldn't. Dag was right, he was fit, he was a navigator, this was what he did.

'Nothing,' he sighed. 'There's no problem, it was just a bit of a surprise that's all. So, you've got a new crew?'

Douglas sighed. 'Not exactly.'

'Not exactly?'

'No. That's why I need you. Another reason.'

'I don't follow.'

Dag smiled in the darkness. 'You're an officer. You're allowed in the officers' mess. I'm not. Most of the spare bods are officers, I need you to round them up.'

Roland stared across at the mess building, then back at his friend. 'Dag, I'm only just back. I've been away weeks. I may not know anyone.'

'Roly,' said Dag quietly. 'I'm stuck on 29. It's horrible, I'm on edge every day. I can't stand it much longer, waiting to see if I get rostered. Please, can you try? I need to get this last trip done.'

Roland continued to stare at him. Whether dawn was starting, or his eyes had adjusted better to the darkness, he could see Dag better now. He'd changed since he'd last seen him, he looked thinner, older, his face gaunt, lined, his hair needed a cut. He looked wounded, cornered, on the edge.

He couldn't know that the friend he had turned to could provide the last push to tip him over.

'Yes,' Roland said. 'All right, I'll do it. I'll find you a crew.'

LMF 7

'Whilst ATKINSON-GRIEVE was recruiting his crew, W/C HARVEY consulted with senior squadron officers and the senior Medical Officer as to the pilot's suitability to fly. No serious objections were raised'

26/1/44 7.57 am

'Alan?'

Squadron-leader Harvey's reverie was broken by a knock on the door. He turned away from the window where he'd been staring out into the darkness.

'Doc,' he said. He nodded at the file the man was carrying. 'Is that the malingerers report?'

'Alan, really,' said the doctor, pulling a face.

'Don't look at me like that, you know it's true.' Harvey held out his hand. 'What have we got today? Any gaps in the crews?'

'Just one. Charleston's crew is down a bomb aimer, he's got a bad toothache. Other than a few bad colds and a dose of clap amongst the mechanics, we're okay for tonight.'

This time Harvey frowned. 'The clap? What's his name? He needs to go on a charge.'

'Oh, come on, Alan, give the boy a break.'

'A break? Getting a dose is a voluntary thing. It's stupid, damages the war effort. And I'm the CO, don't question my authority.'

'Of course,' said the doctor. 'Sorry, sir.'

Harvey sat down and held his hands up. He sighed. 'No, Doc, it's me that should be apologising. Didn't mean to snap. You know what it's like on days like this.'

'Yes, Alan, I know.'

Harvey looked over the file, made notes and then passed it back to the doctor who he expected would then leave. He didn't.

'Is there something else?'

'Well, yes. I've just seen Saunders.'

'Oh right, he's back is he? Hopefully he's learned how to get out of a machine properly whilst he's been away.'

'Come on, Alan, I'm sure he didn't rip his shoulder on purpose.'

Harvey just grunted a reply. He had no wish to start another argument. 'He hasn't officially reported in yet, don't know why,' he said. 'He should have.'

'I saw him with Dag,' said the doctor. 'Maybe that's why.'

'Maybe,' said Harvey.

'Wonder what they were talking about.'

'Oh there's no mystery there,' said Harvey. 'Dag will have recruited him for his crew.'

'His crew? Dag's flying?'

'Well, he will be if he can get other people to fly with him. He came to me this morning asking me to give him a plane so he can finish his tour.'

'You said yes?' The doctor looked aghast.

Harvey shrugged. 'Why shouldn't I? He's a rostered pilot on the squadron, pilots fly. What possible objection can there be?'

'Where do I start?' said the doctor. 'Fundamentally, his mental stability is questionable. Are you really going to risk a crew with him?'

'Doc, you're pushing things again. Are you really questioning my judgement?' Harvey could tell from the doctor's face that he was so pressed on. 'Look, he's got the right to try and complete his tour. It may not happen, I've told him he's got to put his own crew together, and he's got to do it by ten. Chances are he won't manage it, everyone knows what he's like.'

'But what if he does? What then?'

Harvey shrugged again. 'Then so what? He won't get anyone who's any real use from the spares, that's why they're spares in the first place, because everyone's found out that they're useless.'

'That's a bit bloody harsh, Alan.'

'It's the bloody truth, Doc. This war is bloody harsh, too. Look, whatever happens, we win. Dag gets back, he does his tour, he gets his posting, we get rid of him. If they don't get back what've we lost? A crock aircraft and a crock crew.' Harvey smiled. 'Don't look at me like that, Doc. All I'm doing is making your job easier, you know that's true.'

The doctor stared at him for a few second then saluted.

'Sir,' he said quietly and left without another word.

LMF 8

'Mid-upper Gunner - F/L PASCOE (dob 3/5/1922, 12 missions)'

26/1/1944 8.03 am

Gerry had found a table on his own, notebook and pen placed carefully by his cutlery ready for the inspiration that would surely come back one day soon. Poetry, he told himself, could not be forced, it had to be allowed to develop and flow out when it was ready.

It obviously wasn't.

'Eggs and bacon, sir?'

The WAAF had broad, generous lips, bright scarlet and moist with newly applied lipstick. She had tightly curled, permed, near black hair and a cheeky, knowing grin.

Automatically, Gerry returned the smile with one of his own, albeit fleetingly as he was watching the door to the mess.

'Yes, thanks,' he said.

The WAAF was not for leaving anytime soon. 'It's looking like it's going to be better weather today,' she said. 'I never know if that's good or bad, do you, sir?'

Gerry broke his vigil and stared at her. What did she mean?

His puzzlement clearly showed.

'I mean for tonight, sir. Better weather means that you might be flying. If you're going of course. Oh…' She raised her hand to her mouth and looked around her. It was clearly a theatrical gesture. 'Silly me, we're not supposed to gossip, are we? I can't help it, I get to know you boys and like you.' She gave a little frown and a shrug, again the gesture did not look natural to Gerry, this was something she'd rehearsed, but why? 'Oh, not that I do know you, of course, sir, save from serving you at mealtimes like this. It's not like we're going out, is it?'

'Robinson! Get a move on, there's other people that need serving.'

'Sorry, ma'am,' the girl called, then turned her back on her supervisor and scowled. 'Witch,' she muttered. 'Still, I'd better get on or she'll have my guts.' She began to walk away then stopped. 'Oh, I forgot, drink?'

Gerry had been distracted by two new entrants to the mess, both tall and blonde, one very familiar and the other not. 'Drink?' he repeated.

'Port and lemon, if you're asking!' The WAAF giggled archly.

'Sorry?' He looked up at her, uncomprehending.

She raised her eyebrows in mock exasperation. 'I meant did you want tea?' she said.

'Oh, yes. Please,' he said, wishing she would go away. He wanted to wave Adam over and for him to bring his companion with him. Now he was closer the man looked vaguely familiar. Whoever he was, he made Gerry's heart skip. He was slim, lithe and gorgeous. He moved in a gentle, almost poetic fashion, flowing into the mess like music filling the room.

'Coming right up,' said the WAAF.

He only distantly heard her as Adam had seen him and was heading in his direction although, sadly, on his own and, as in recent weeks, looking more sullen than Gerry would have liked, as if spending time in Gerry's company was more of a chore than a pleasure. Did his friend really think that way? Surely not, he was getting over-sensitive again, seeing things that weren't there. It hadn't been the first time he'd done that.

'Morning, Adam, sleep well?' he said.

'Yes,' said Adam, sitting down.

'There's eggs on the menu. You know what that means, don't you?'

'Yeah, of course I bloody well do,' Adam muttered. Gerry saw him look across at the other tables, there was some envy mixed with anger in his gaze. Gerry could guess why.

The other tables were sat in crews. Men that banded together, drank together, ate together, flew together. Crews like theirs used to be.

Theirs had been a whole officer crew, which meant they had all eaten in the same mess. Happy days, if trips to Happy Valley could ever be that.

Adam and Gerry and Peter, Graham, Angus, Johnny and Alan. There had been seven of them and now there were just two. Five faces were missing, five whose features Gerry now struggled to remember but who he would never forget. Five men who Adam blamed him for killing.

Gerry blinked the moisture from his eyes and looked for something, anything else to look at. Then he saw the new-comer again. He <u>did</u> know him, he remembered now, Ronald? No, Roland, yes that was it.

He looked confused. Gerry wished he would head towards their table.

LMF 9

'F/L SAUNDERS recruited both air gunners and the bomb aimer from the officers' mess during breakfast.'

26/1/1944 8.07 am

R oland had not prepared himself for the mess, he had landed in the middle of the hubbub before he knew it.

It was almost overwhelming, like stepping into a waking nightmare, taking him right back to where he had been before his accident. In any other circumstances he would have skipped breakfast and delayed plunging into the pool until he was ready.

Now he had to swim to survive.

He blinked, uncertain as to where to go. The noise was confusing, the babble of young, male voices was incessant, and others thought intruded.

Firstly, Dag. He had asked him to help out of friend-ship, loyalty, fidelity but Roland was acting out of guilt.

But there was something worse. Since joining up he had been able to convince himself that he was being carried by the tide, swept by the current, the need to fight in a just war against Fascism. It was not his decision to take up arms. His country had asked him and he'd responded. Now, though, was different, he was the recruiter, he could not fool himself it was otherwise.

He should turn around and walk out of the mess, the airfield, of the squadron, the war and, therefore, out of the

41

freedom he enjoyed.

Away from Connie though, that would happen too. He'd lose her.

He started walking again, away from the thick of the action, away from the most crowded tables towards the fringes where the men sat in one's and twos. They would be the spare bods, the airmen without a regular crew, those trying to force breakfast down past dry mouths into churning stomachs, those who faced the agony of doubt, of anticipation, fear and hope as to whether they would be rostered to fill any gaps in the crew lists.

When he had arrived from the HCU he had envied thembecause they could sit things out. Later he understood better and pitied them; they had no certainty, they were condemned without knowing their execution date.

He tried to find a familiar face. Who did he know? So many strangers, how could that be in just six weeks? Then he saw a chap who was looking towards Roland. Did he know him? He thought he might. What was his name?

A WAAF was just leaving their table. She he did know, who didn't? Mavis Robinson, flirty Mavis, the officer hunter.

The irony was obvious. She wanted their bodies, their skills, what they brought to the table and would flirt, tease and entrap them for her own ends.

Just like him.

Visions of his father and brother's disapproving faces came to him. The pain in his shoulder returned, his mouth was dry, his tongue thick. Would he be able to speak at all?

'Excuse me?' he said to the pair, surprising himself with his voice. It was honey-sweet, gentle, enticing. 'Is this seat taken?'

The executioner sat and tried to suppress his shame and disgust in himself.

LMF 10

'…Rear Gunner - F/L TAYLOR (dob 1/8/1920, 12 missions).'

26/1/44 8.10 am

Adam's mind was elsewhere when the newcomer introduced himself and sat down at the table.

The name did register though. Roland Saunders, Roly who wasn't at all Roly-poly. Lean, fit and athletic, he had the air of a schoolteacher or don about him.

Just Gerry's type.

Gerry, bloody Gerry. Poor Gerry. He couldn't help the way he was, could he? It was his nature, like asking a sheep not to be a sheep, Adam should try not to be hard on him. But then *he* couldn't help being that way either, it *was* Gerry's fault that they missed the trip with the rest of the boys.

But then, that meant that the pair of them were still alive. The seven that went, their five friends and the two spares, all died. Gerry's 'adventure' had saved them. It condemned them too, sentencing them to survivor's guilt. The one thought: how good were the two chaps that had replaced them? Gerry and Adam had been the crew's last line of defence. What if it was a fighter that had got them that night? Perhaps he and Gerry might have been able to see it, shout a warning, fight it off?

Whatever, they were doubly condemned, now spare bods themselves. It was agony waiting, seeing if you'd be called to fly. A month it had been, more in fact, thirty-three days. The squadron had flown fourteen trips in that time. If he'd flown them all he'd have done twenty-six, four short of a complete tour. He'd be almost done, due a break which meant he'd have got to see Sarah and the baby that was due next month. Their first, longed for in peace but, exquisitely cruelly, conceived in the 48 hours leave after the HCU.

Twenty-six, if he'd flown them all but he'd actually done just three and one of those was an abort that didn't count. He'd never finish, he'd never see his son or daughter, he knew it, he just did.

Thanks to Gerry.

But then, thanks to Gerry, he wasn't dead.

Mavis was back, flirting again. What a little fool, wasn't she blind to the fact that Gerry was flirting too but not with her?

'So you two are gunners?' Saunders was saying.

'We certainly are. Mid-upper and tail gunner respect-ively. You know Adam don't you, Roland? Adam Taylor?'

'By sight, yes,' said Saunders, holding out his hand to Adam. 'Weren't you in-'

'Yes,' said Adam quickly, taking the hand. 'They bought it just before Christmas.'

'Ah, right, sorry,' said Saunders. 'Look, I won't beat about the bush, I've been asked to put a crew together for tonight.'

'What crew are you in?' Adam said. 'You've been on sick leave, haven't you?'

'This is a new crew, an extra machine.'

'Well, that sounds great, doesn't it, Adam?' Gerry was beaming. 'Back in a crew again, back in the line full-time.'

'Wait, I didn't say...' Saunders began, but someone on the table behind leaned over and interrupted.

'I say, that's a good show. A spare machine, a new crew? Have you got a bomb-aimer?'

Adam groaned inwardly. Howard, the mess bore, hopeless and pompous, avoided by everyone where possible.

'Well, no we haven't, but...' said Saunders.

'Then I'm your man. Count me in.' Howard picked his plate up, got up and came and sat with them.

'Right. Fine,' said Saunders. By the look on his face, Adam suspected that he, too, knew Howard's reputation. 'That's four of us then, five with the pilot - if you're in of course.'

'Oh yes, of course we're in, aren't we, Adam?'

Adam was already on his feet. He had no desire to spend any more time with Howard than he needed to. He'd skip breakfast, write to Sarah.

'Yes, why not?' he said.

As he left, he heard Howard ask who the pilot was.

LMF 11

Burt paused briefly outside the sergeant's mess, lit another cigarette and, ignoring the cold, walked out onto the airfield.

He kept away from the hangars, from people, and headed around the perimeter road. Simply walking was helping. He was always quick to tell anyone what he felt about the English climate, that it was like the rest of the country: grey and always damp. It didn't compare to the vast soaring skies of Australia.

He missed the heat, the smell of eucalyptus, the blue haze it brought to the air, the rustle of dry grass and the thunder of rain - proper rain - on a tin roof, a proper roof. Even the rain here was depressing, slow, slight, timid and tortuous. Still, though, there was something about the cold, misty mornings in the Fens that cleared the head, something about the flatlands that calmed the soul.

His thoughts now were of the faraway land of Sydney and Bathurst, how it would be there right now. Here he was in the depths of a dark winter, there it would be blistering, brilliant summer. It would be evening, the end of the day. Where would Mags be, out of hospital with the kids or still there, in a bed, surrounded by strangers? In pain?

What if she was? What if she never left? What would happen then? What would he do? What *could* he do?

He had arrived at the point where the tracks left the

perimeter road. They cut deep furrows through the grass to-wards the fence, new wire marking the spot where it had been broken down and then replaced a week or so later. Burt looked back across the airfield, it was getting lighter, he was halfway between two of the dispersed hardstandings, each with a Halifax on it. He turned back towards the fence, re-membering the view from up there when he'd found himself on the grass.

At the time, he'd no memory of exactly how he'd got there and the memory had not come back. But then his mem-ory about the whole day, 25th November 1943, was very patchy.

He walked down to the fence, took his hands out of his pockets and hooked them into the wire mesh. The bite of cold nipping his skin was painfully soothing He took in the other sensations, the metallic tang of the new metal, the acrid af-tertone of the fresh concrete posts but everything was dom-inated by two things; the stench of burning and of aviation fuel.

It was still too dark to see properly but Burt knew that out there, amongst the churned-up fields, separated by a few hundred yards, were two black, stinking holes where the trembling marshland had swallowed F- Freddie and J-Jack and their 13 men.

It had taken two weeks to dig out the last of the bodies from the peat, at least that was what they had been told, there had been mutters that they'd just given up and packed the coffins with a mixture of what they'd found, human and rocks, and left the rest to the fens. Whatever, this was the place where the 14th man, the engineer of F-Freddie felt closest to his mates, not in the local churchyard, but here, right here.

He had no idea why he hadn't joined them, God only knew, and he wasn't telling. He'd woken up on the ground, shrouded in silk, tangled in nylon, sticky from the blood flow-ing from his scalp lacerated by the perspex windscreen he'd clearly gone through. He'd sat up, fought for vision and found himself bathed in a ruddy glow that he didn't then understand but now knew to be the funeral pyres of his mates and the tyro crew who'd collided with them on final approach.

All after coming safely back from Berlin.

It was so unfair.

He cleared his throat.

'G'day, cobbers,' he said. 'Sorry to bother you but I got a problem and I could do with a bit of advice. I know you blokes won't mind.'

He had a long talk with them. They didn't say anything but were good listeners. Only they could understand.

When he got back to the barracks there was a telegram waiting for him.

LMF 12

'The remaining crew members were obtained from the Sergeants' mess at the same time.'

26/1/44 8.38 am

A wall of noise and a wave of heat carrying a melange of smells - tea, milk, burnt toast and fried food - greeted John as he walked into the sergeants' mess.

Four long rows of trestle tables and benches packed the room and men sat shoulder-to-shoulder, jostling for space. Hassled looking WAAFs and auxiliary staff, all women, navigated their way along the aisles bearing trays from which they unloaded full cups and plates and reloaded with used ones.

John had hesitated before finally stepping inside. He'd been put off by the crowds and the atmosphere and had feigned interest in the notice boards outside, reading everything, official and personal alike until he could put off the moment no longer. Within, committed, he stood blinking, uncertain, wondering where he could sit.

One man, dark hair neatly brylcreemed and combed, stared at him then nudged his companion with his elbow.

'Eh, Don?' he said loudly.

'Yeah?' said the burly, blonde-haired giant opposite him.

'You remember tellin' us about that milkround you used to 'ave'

'Yeah?'

'Well, I think one o'them lonely housewives has sent your lad over to see if you're comin' back!'

The roar of laughter was largely aimed in John's direction. He almost fled but one of the older men turned as the laughter died down and patted the bench next to him.

'C'mon, son, pull up a pew,' he said. 'I'm Harry.'

'John,' said John as he sat.

'New in?'

'Yes. Last night.'

'More flak-fodder,' said the Brylcreemed one. 'Bleedin' 'ell though, you could do with a bit more meat on you. What are you, about six stone?'

'I don't...'

'And 'ow old are you? 'Bout 12?'

'I'm 18,' John realised he was flushing.

'Yer, 'course you are, son. Mabel, Mabel! Be a love and gis us one of yer teas and some toast for the lad. He needs feedin' up.'

Tea and toast with some strawberry jam appeared in front of him. John sipped the tea, it was too sweet and milky for his liking, but he said nothing and drank it nonetheless.

'Looks like we're on tonight,' said someone on John's left.

'Yeah,' said someone else. 'Where do you reckon? Berlin?'

'Nah, it'll be Happy Valley. Gotta be.'

'What crew you in?' said Harry. 'Where's the rest of your mob, in the officers' mess?'

'No, there's just me,' said John. 'I did have a crew at the

HCU but then I had to go and have an operation.'

'Why, hadn't your balls dropped?' said Brylcreem and, before John could explain about his ingrowing toenails, added; 'Oh look out, Lord Muck's 'ere. Keep your 'eads down.'

But, instead, everyone's head turned towards the door where an intense, dark-haired man wearing pilot's wings on his chest, stood, though, John noticed, they all looked away again quickly. John didn't and, moments later, made eye contact.

The man walked up to their table.

'I'm looking for a crew for tonight. Gunners, an engineer and a sparky.'

'Sparky?' said John.

'Don't act dumb,' said the man. 'A radio-operator.'

'Oh, right,' said John. 'I'm a...er...sparky and - ow!'

Someone had kicked him under the table.

'Are you? Not in a crew?'

John barely had time to shake his head.

'Right, you'll do. First briefing is in twenty-five minutes. See you there. Oh, what's your name, I'll need it for admin.'

'Hiley. John Hiley.'

'Right, good. Anyone else?'

No one said a word.

The pilot gave an irritated sigh and moved on to the next table.

Brylcreem shook his head sadly and muttered something that sounded like, 'You fuckin' stupid little bastard.'

LMF 13

'The crew attended the general briefings as normal prior to the raid.'

26/1/44 9.50 am

'Gentlemen, that will be all for now. We will resume at 1630 hours for the target briefing.'

The sound of a few hundred chairs being pushed back and the babble of voices began even before the intelligence officer had completed his sentence. The main topic of conversation was predictable; the identity of the target that lay shrouded beneath the cloth covering the board at the very centre of the stage.

Douglas didn't care. He was only concerned about the time and his crew, especially the one who was missing.

The gunners looked okay although one was rather too talkative and eager to please whilst the other was quiet and seemed distracted. Roland, of course, he knew. Sure he had his problems but, as a navigator, he was sound. The other pair though, they were another matter.

The radio operator was a sprog, he looked permanently terrified, afraid to open his mouth which, considering his trade, was a major problem.

He wished that the bomb aimer was as reticent. Douglas had taken an instant dislike to Howard.

'They all call me Leslie, you know, after the film star,' he'd introduced himself oilily. 'I don't know why, after all I'm far better looking - and alive!' He laughed at his own humour.

'I'm Terrence really. But, of course, it will be 'Sir' to you, Sergeant.'

'You'll be what I fucking choose to call you, Terry,' Douglas had replied.

'Damn you, I'm and officer! I outrank -'

'Not in the air, you don't. I'm in command.'

'Well, we're not in the air now are we, and -'

'Stop, please, the pair of you.' Roland had stepped between them. 'This is not doing any of us any good, is it? Dag, Leslie, come on, we've got to work together. We need to be a team.'

'Oh yes, we all need to be friends and love one another, don't we? Keep your beliefs to yourself, thank you.'

Douglas had regretted the words as soon as they had left his mouth. Roland blinked like he'd been slapped.

'Well, yes, but...er...' he had begun but, at that point, the briefing had started.

The bad blood and hot words had been left to lie and fester. Roland had lapsed into contemplative thoughtfulness whilst Howard, soft and dumpy, ran his finger through his thinning hair. Douglas saw that he made no notes and didn't seem to pay much attention to the stage, preferring to glower at the pilot and mutter to himself.

'I can't see why they can't tell us the target now,' Douglas heard him say.

'It's security, old chap,' Pascoe had whispered back. 'Wouldn't want word about the target getting back to Jerry, would we? It's hot enough over there as it is.'

'It just shows a lack of trust,' Howard had muttered. 'We don't get enough time to prepare for the really important part of the mission.'

Now the briefing was over, Douglas did not get up and

join the exodus. He stayed where he was and watched the bomb aimer leave. He shook his head, he wouldn't do, he just wouldn't.

But it would be all right. All he had to do was fly the raid, drop the bombs and get back, then it would all be over and done and he'd be all right too.

He noticed that Roland had hung back. Good, he guessed that he wanted a word. But then he saw that the sprog hadn't left either.

'Yes?' he said. 'What do you want.'

'I...er...was just wondering...er...what-'

'We inspect the aircraft, of course. Check over your station. Make damn certain that everything works.'

'Yes, but...'

'Hiley, just wait outside and I'll show you where to go,' said Roland gently. 'I won't be long, I just want a word with Dag.'

'Oh right, yes, thank you, sir.'

Douglas watched him leave.

'God, what have I done?' he muttered. 'Mind you, at least he's better than Howard. Where did you find him? Do you know anything about him?'

'No, Dag, sorry. I can ask around though.'

'What's the point? It's a bit late now.' He looked at his watch. 'In fact, it probably doesn't matter what shit you've collected for a crew, I've got to see Harvey now and we've still got no engineer. It's all probably a bust anyway. Oh, did you want to talk to me about something?'

'Well...Dag, I...' Roland began but Douglas cut him off.

'Look, forget it, I haven't the time for small talk now. You might as well go to the plane. Probably a waste of time but... Anyway, see you there.'

He left before Roland had time to say anything else.

LMF 14

'**S**it down there, Burt. I'll have a quick word with the old man. I'm sure we can sort something out for you.'

Burt only vaguely heard the adjutant's voice. His heart was racing, his breathing short and erratic.

'I've got to see him,' he muttered. 'I've got to get going, get back to the kids. Please, just let me in, he'll understand.'

He stepped towards the door but felt his shoulders grasped gently but firmly and him being pulled back. There was a brief flash of anger. For a moment he was back in NSW, if anyone there had laid a hand on him, at work, on the street, at the cricket or in a bar, he would have laid them out. He raised his fists but then the soft voice of the adjutant, a silver-haired Great War veteran, got through.

'Steady now, Burt old son, there's no need for that is there? You just take a seat and let me sort things out for you.'

Burt allowed himself to be placed in one of the chairs beside the secretary's desk whilst the adjutant tapped lightly on the Squadron Leader's door.

'Yes, what is it? Colin, I'm busy. Is this urgent?'

The voices became muffled as the adjutant stepped into the office but were still clearly audible.

'It is. It's about Burt Harrison.'

'Who?'

'Sergeant Harrison? The engineer on F-Freddie?'

'What about him?'

The door was closed, leaving Burt alone with the WAAF manning the desk. She smiled at him sympathetically but then looked away. She was young, barely more than a girl, what would she know? Burt closed his eyes, trying to get his breathing under control. It was unbelievable, Mags was dying, how could she be dying? What would the kids do? How would they be taking it? Did they know?

The outer office door was flung open.

'I need to see the old man.'

Burt opened his eyes. It was a pilot, a sergeant like him, brisk, on edge, eyes gleaming and already halfway to the door.

'No, sergeant you can't, he's with someone,' said the WAAF, standing and barring his way to the door.

'But he said he wanted to see me at ten.'

'Well, you'll have to wait. He's busy.'

The pilot gave an exasperated sigh. 'Oh, for God's sake.' He looked at his watch. 'He'd better not be too long, I'm running out of time. You're not waiting as well, are you?'

For the first time the pilot had looked at Burt.

'Yes,' he said.

The pilot swore and sat down next to Burt.

Burt knew him. They'd never spoken but he knew him. A pom, a pom with a posh girlfriend and a massive chip on his shoulder. Spoke like an officer but wasn't one.

Mags. Oh God, Mags.

'Bloody hell, Colin, really? I'm trying to fight a war here, you can't be serious!'

The words were muffled by the closed office door but

were quite clear. Burt couldn't hear the reply but heard the Squadron Leader quite clearly.

'No. Absolutely not. If we give it to one, we'll have to give it to the rest, and then where would we be? It can't be done. Is he outside?'

The office door opened. Both Burt and the pilot got to their feet.

'Harrison,' said Harvey. 'Look, I'm really sorry about your wife but my hands are tied. You're an experienced man, I can't let the likes of you go. You do understand, don't you?'

'Yes, sir.'

Burt felt the room spin. He thought he would faint.

'Good man. And for goodness' sake, smarten yourself up. You're a mess. Can't let your standards slip just because you've got a bit of bad news from home. Don't let the side down, eh?'

'No sir,' he muttered.

He saw Harvey's eyes flick to the pilot.

'Dag, what do you want? Oh yes, your deadline. Well, have you managed it? Come inside, make it quick.'

Harvey and the pilot went into the inner office.

'Sorry, Burt.' the adjutant said, but the engineer was already walking away.

LMF 15

'W1263 is a Halifax MKII Srs 1A, built by the Rootes group and supplied new to the squadron in April 1943. It had completed 57 missions and had a good serviceability record.'

26/1/44 10.15 am

'**H**ow long are we going to have to hang around here? It's bloody freezing.'

John saw the gunners exchange glances. He could guess why, the bomb aimer, Howard, had done nothing but complain since they had come together. He was talking to the navigator, Saunders who the others also deferred to. He did seem to be one of life's natural leaders. John wondered why he didn't have a higher rank.

'Just give Dag a few more minutes,' Saunders said, looking at his watch. 'He'll be along shortly.'

Howard was obviously not convinced. 'I'll believe it when I see it. This whole thing's a mare's nest, it's not going to happen.'

'Of course it will,' said Saunders.

'Oh come on, you said he needed a complete crew and we've got no engineer. Even if we get one, we're behind the game. The engineer's supposed to be checking the machine over now. Who's going to do that?'

Saunders folded his arms and turned to look at the admin block. 'Dag'll find someone, I'm sure.'

'Well I'm not and we all know why don't we? The man's

a jumped-up guttersnipe. What's all this double-barrelled business about? He's nothing, a sergeant, putting on airs and -'

'Oh put a sock in it, Leslie,' sighed Taylor. 'He's a good pilot. He's got the DFM, didn't you see his medal ribbon?'

'If he's so good, why hasn't he got a crew? He had one, didn't he? Why didn't he finish his tour with them?'

'And why didn't you finish yours with your original crew, Leslie?' Taylor's face was impassive as he stared at Howard.

'That's...I...that's beside the point,' said Howard. 'He's got all of our lives in his hands. Anyway, we shouldn't be discussing things in front of the other ranks.' John realised he was talking about him.

'Let's stop the bickering,' said Saunders, looking at his watch. 'Come on, let's go and look the machine over. We can at least do our own station checks, we don't need an engineer for that.'

Howard gave a snort of derision. 'What's the point? We won't be going anywhere.'

'Look, we might as well keep busy. Have you really got anything better to do?'

'Well, no,' said Howard. 'But surely we'll need a car to take us to dispersal?'

'No, actually,' said Saunders, pointing. 'It's that one there.'

They all turned and looked.

'That?' said Pascoe at last. 'C-Charlie? I thought that was on the way to the scrapper.'

'No, it's Watkins old machine. He's just got a new one from the depot. Come on, I'm sure it's not that bad.'

He set off walking. His confident stride had an instant effect on everyone, they all followed, even Howard had stopped grumbling.

At least until they reached the machine.

The five men stood in a loose semi-circle around it. No one said a word for a full minute which told John that their impressions were the same as his. He was used to flying old, tired machines at the HCU and, prior to that, during training, but this was the most battered aircraft he had ever seen.

The perspex of the gun turrets was yellow with age, that of the cockpit a mixture of old and new panels. The camouflage browns and greens of the upper surfaces were faded and scuffed, the black undersides scarred and scratched, silver showing through in innumerable places. The inspection panels and service hatches bore the marks where screwdrivers and wrenches in dozens of different hands over many months had undone, replenished and replaced, most were dented, some looked to have been salvaged off other machines. Just beneath the cockpit a new aluminium sheet had been pop-riveted over the existing skin and roughly painted black.

John stared at this point because he knew, behind that, was roughly where the radio operator sat. If that was repaired battle damage, what had happened to the man who had been there during that mission?

'Fuck me,' said Taylor at last. 'Watkins doesn't look after his toys, does he?'

Saunders was staring up at the nose where bomb symbols were painted just below the cockpit. John looked too. There were six rows of ten bombs, and two on the row beneath.

'She'll be all right,' he said. 'She's done a lot of missions.'

'So's an old whore who's past it and no one wants to ride anymore,' said Howard. 'And that's just what she looks like.'

'That's enough, Howard,' said Saunders. 'Come on.'

Reluctantly, the crew started to climb into C-Charlie.

LMF 16

'All of the crew volunteered to fly on the mission.'

26/1/44 10.17 am

The slamming of the office door rattled the panes in the windows and brought the squadron leader to his feet.

'Sergeant!' he yelled. 'How dare you? Get back -'

The adjutant raised his hands placatingly. 'Leave it, David. The lad's highly strung.'

'Highly strung? I'd string the bastard up if I could. I gave him a chance. It's not my fault that everyone knows his reputation. No wonder he couldn't get people to fly with him.'

The adjutant picked up the hand-written list the pilot had handed over 'Oh I don't know. He did pretty well in a couple of hours.'

'Saunders did well you mean. Dag got one taker from the Sergeants' mess, a sprog who couldn't possibly know him. That says legions, doesn't it? Let's have a look at the rest.' Harvey held out his hand, the adjutant passed over the list. 'Hmm, I wouldn't miss any of these, though.'

'That's a bit harsh, David.'

'Is it? Our wavering Quaker? And Howard? He's bloody useless, the worst bombadier in the group let alone the squadron. I suppose Taylor's all right. As for Pascoe...well.' He tossed the list on the desk and ran his fingers through his hair. 'I really could do without this. Why do I get such hassle from the sergeants in this squadron? First that bloody antipodean wanting me to put the war on hold whilst he sorts out his personal problems, and now bloody Dag. What's wrong with them? Why can't they just obey orders? And what's Dag doing as a sergeant anyway? He's from a decent background. Damn the man, I really thought I could get rid of him this time.'

'You could just transfer him out.'

'He wouldn't have it. Nor would the ministry, given who his old man is.' Harvey sighed. He picked up the list, then looked at the door. 'Wait a minute, what an idiot I am. The answer's right in front of us.'

'What do you mean?'

'Harrison! He's an engineer, isn't he?'

'Well, yes, but come on, David, you can't be serious.'

'Why not?'

'His mind's hardly likely to be on the job, is it? Wife dying and all that?'

'Exactly, he's going to be useless to us. Let him fly with Dag, do him a deal. Tell him if he does this favour for us and we'll look again at this compassionate leave request of his.'

The adjutant opened his mouth. 'I don't think...'

'It will be fine. Two birds with one stone, ideal. Off you go and put it to him and then get word to Dag if he says yes, which, of course, he will.' Harvey sat back and breathed a sigh of relief. 'Thank God that's sorted. Go on, chop chop.'

'Yes, sir,' said the adjutant, his face wooden.

LMF 17

26/1/44 10.20 am

Douglas did not know where he was going, he just wanted to be alone.

He bumped blindly into a couple of people - he didn't know who - and didn't stay to find out but was aware of voices behind him.

'Bloody idiot.'

'Leave him. He's crazy, everyone knows that.'

He's crazy.

Everyone knows that.

He's crazy.

The words went around and round in his head, swirling, mixing and deepening his anger and frustration. Was he crazy? Was he? It was what he feared, dreaded, half accepted. Daily he could feel himself coming apart, he had to fight against it, to drag himself back from the edge. The nights were the worst, those never-ending sleepless hours before dawn when his thoughts raced and his fears of the inevitability of insanity grew.

Something needed to change, he needed to change. He needed to get out of here.

He was getting out. He had a chance and now it had been snatched away.

He stumbled his way through the frigid morning,

turned right and then right again, down between two buildings. He stopped, fumbled for his cigarettes and matches, the cold numbing his fingers which were, in any case, shaking with emotion. He managed to get a cigarette out of the packet but dropped the matches, the half open box spilling its contents.

'Fuck it! Fuck it!' he yelled.

'Dag?'

He scrambled around in the dirt, forcing, with some difficulty, the matches back into the box.

'Dag, are you all right?'

His hands didn't want to obey him, he had to force them to grasp the box, to take a match out, to strike it - or try to, it splintered without lighting.

He flung it and the matches away.

'Fuck it, fuck it, fuck everything!'

He closed his eyes, breathing heavily.

He had a notion of a light touch, a feather of breath on his cheek. There was the scent of flowers, how could there be flowers at this time of year? He really was crazy.

A rasp, a bitter but familiar smell of chemicals, phosphorus melding into wood smoke. Though his eyes were still closed an image formed, lips, pink, sensuously, suggestively closing around the unlit end, drawing, sucking in the smoke, kindling it to life.

In his mind she took it from her lips and offered it up to his. He wished it could be real.

And then it was.

'Dag,' she said. 'Take it easy. Calm down.'

He wanted so much to hold her, he needed to embrace her, to feel her close to him. Everything was alright then, it always was. He had enough control, though, not to. He knew he shouldn't, not in public, not on the base because he was just a sergeant and she an officer.

So he did nothing but draw the tobacco smoke deep inside him, letting the nicotine work its magic.

At last he was able to speak.

'Connie, darling,' he said. 'It's so good to see you.'

LMF 18

'The aircraft was checked over by the crew on the morning of the 26th and no problems were found.'

26/1/44 10.40 am

'You all right, John?'

The voice made Hiley jump. He'd been staring at the inner skin of the aircraft. 'Er, yes, sorry sir. I was just trying to work out what to do.'

It was Saunders the navigator. He had come back from his position just behind the bomb aimer in the nose of the aircraft to John's, virtually under the pilot's seat.

'There's no need for the 'sir' on the aircraft, John, it's Roland or Saunders, whatever you prefer.' He came across to the radio operator's table. 'You need to check that everything is working and whatever you need is there, and learn where it is so you can find it in the dark. If you find anything that's u/s or even looks like it might be dicky, then this is the time to find it. Out over Hunland is too late.'

'Right, sir, yes sir.'

'Roland, remember John,' said Saunders.

'Sorry, Roland, yes, sir.'

'Just work methodically through everything. Do it your own way but check everything at least twice. It may seem overkill, but it will help to keep your mind occupied and not dwelling on tonight.'

'Yes sir, I mean, Roland.'

John could not help but glance back at what his eye had constantly been drawn to, the patch of fresh aluminium on the skin of the aircraft to his left. There were also scars on the metal table in front of him and a chunk taken out of the casing of the VHF set.

Saunders seemed to read his thoughts. 'Don't worry, John. Lightning doesn't strike twice in the same place, does it?' He patted John's shoulder. 'You'll be fine.'

'Roland? Is that you?'

The call came from further back in the aircraft.

'Yes, Gerry, what is it?'

The gunner came forward. 'What's going on? We've not been rearmed, we've no ammunition.'

'Give it time, it's early -'

'We're also not bombed up, or fueled, in fact no-one seems to be coming anywhere near us. Are we on or not?'

'As far as I know we are,' said Saunders. 'It is a bit strange though. How are the turrets?'

'Like the rest of this crate, worn out and knackered.'

'This is bloody stupid. I said it was.' Howard had also come back to the rear of the aircraft. 'No engineer and no pilot either. Where is he?'

'I'm sure they'll both be along in a minute, Leslie,' said Saunders. 'In the meantime all we can do is do our jobs.'

'With what? This crap? The bombsight's so old I can barely see through it. It's a shambles, an utter, bloody shambles.'

John's head was reeling. This wasn't like training. Was it always this bad?

'Hey, what the 'ell you lot doin' in 'ere?'

The voice came from behind Howard, John guessed that it must be somebody in the forward escape hatch.

'Eh, Fred,' the person called, 'There's a crew in 'ere.'

'Wot they doin' in that heap?' came a more distant reply.

'Who the hell do you think you're talking to?' Howard said, his voice pompous and angry. 'Don't you salute an officer?'

John heard Saunders mutter, 'God give me strength,' then, more loudly as he stepped forward, 'Leslie, go back to your station, I'll deal with this.'

'But, the man's insubordinate, I should...'

'Go back to your station, please,' said Saunders, his tone still calm. 'Now then, Corporal, I'm glad you're here. We're flying this machine tonight, so we'll need...'

Saunders' voice faded away, John felt the aircraft sway slightly as someone, presumably the navigator, descended the stairs with the mechanic.

John was relieved Saunders was in the crew, he was so calm, he filled people with confidence, even tyros like him.

He started to prepare a checklist and tried not to dwell on had happened to whoever had sat in this seat before.

LMF 19

T he nicotine coursing through his system did wonders to soothe Douglas's frayed nerves. Yet as he calmed it seemed to him that Connie became tenser.

What was wrong? It wasn't the rank thing again was it, her recent promotion? She'd been different since that had happened, become more distant, they'd argued more.

Now was not the time to have another.

He came to attention, saluted. 'Warrant Officer Little,' he said.

She returned his salute, but her discomfort was obvious, she could not look at him, her eyes flicked this way and that.

She didn't want to be seen with him, he thought. Why? Was it the rank thing? Douglas couldn't be sure.

'Can we get out into the open?' she said. 'This look's odd, us sneaking about round here.'

'Er, yes. Of course.' He turned towards the parade ground.

'What's wrong?' she said.

'I'm fine. Now you're back.'

He expected a smile but, instead, she strode past him, straight out onto the parade ground and turned towards the admin building. Momentarily nonplussed, he had to run to catch up with her.

'You've seen Roland?' she said.

'Yes, as soon as he arrived.'

'So that's why you're upset?'

'Yes, of course.'

'I'm sorry.'

'I know, it's the very devil.' '

'We didn't -'

'I really thought this was my chance to get it over and done with.'

Connie stopped walking.

'What do you mean?' she said.

'To get this last trip done, of course, finish my tour. The wait's killing me.'

'A trip? You're flying tonight?'

'Yes, what did -'

'With Roland? He's going with you?'

'Yes - well, he was. It's off. We haven't got a flight engineer and that bastard Harvey won't get me one or give me more time.'

'Oh,' Connie set off walking again.

'Oh?' said Douglas, then hurried to catch up again. 'What did you mean? I thought you knew that was why -'

'It was nothing, forget it.'

'It doesn't look like nothing. It was something else. Something about Roland?'

She stopped again. 'Yes.'

'Is it his family, the Quaker thing?'

'Er...yes...yes, of course.'

'Oh right. Well, he's back now, they can't stop him.'

'No, they can't.'

'Wait.' A thought struck him. 'How did you -'

'He wrote to me, and...' she paused and he saw he glance at something behind him. 'I think you're wanted.' .

He turned to see the squadron adjutant walking towards him.

'Good news, Dag,' he said. 'We've found you an engineer.'

'Yes!' said Douglas and turned to Connie.

But she had already gone.

LMF 20

'All of the specialist departmental briefings took place in the morning prior to the raid…'

26/1/44 10.50 am

'Er, Radio Operator here. Intercom check.'

Adam waited his turn. He listened to the rest of the crew as they replied in the usual order.

'Navigator, loud and clear, John, over.'

Adam waited for the bomb aimer, the next in sequence, to speak.

There was a long pause.

'Mid-upper, check, over,' said Gerry.

That wasn't right, but, then, it had all gone to pot, hadn't it? The sequence should be pilot, engineer, navigator, bomb aimer, then the gunners with him as tail end charlie, of course. The pilot was God-knows where, the engineer was non-existent and, so far as he could see, they were going nowhere in this unarmed, unrefueled, unserviced crock. Why had he agreed to this?

What a duff crate this was, one of the last of the old, field modified series Is, with the crude streamlining over where the front turret had been removed but still with the old, draggy Boulton-Paul turret amidships and without the other weight-saving measures made to give the Halifaxes a chance. All the rest of its breed had either been scrapped, replaced or shot down, how come C-Charlie had escaped? Maybe even the

Germans felt sorry for it.

'Radio operator here again. Bomb aimer, rear gunner, I didn't hear you. Intercom check.'

Adam waited a moment then pressed his intercom switch. 'Sorry, rear gunner here. Check, over.'

Still there was nothing from Howard. Why did they have to have him? This was at least his fourth crew, that spoke legions, didn't it? But, then, was he being unfair, he didn't know Howard personally, everyone deserved a chance. Still, it would be nice to know he was reliable. They needed to work together to survive.

The stakes - his stakes - were so much higher now. Soon, too soon, he would have a son or daughter. Why now? After all these years why did she have to get pregnant now?

At the front of the aircraft he could hear raised voices. Distantly someone said: 'Put your headphones on, Leslie.'

Then his earphones crackled into life.

'--busy, can't you see that? Bloody hell.'

'John needed to do a coms check, Leslie.'

Saunders. A calming influence. At least <u>he</u> was reliable, though the word round the mess was that he came from a family of conchies, that his brother was in jail for refusing to fight and...

'Well it is damn well working.'

'You know these things need to be done, Howard. Anyway, lads, whilst I'm on, just a reminder that the departmental briefings are at quarter-past. We'd all better close up now and get where we need to go.'

'What's the point? This is a total mare's nest.'

'Leave it, Leslie.'

'No, I won't leave it. The two key people, the pilot and the engineer, haven't been here to look the machine over. We've no idea whether this bag of bolts is even airworthy. There's no point going to the briefings. This isn't going to happen.'

'Howard, this machine's done more trips than the rest of us put together,' said Saunders. 'I think that suggests that it's basically airworthy, doesn't it? Dag and the engineer, whoever he gets, can do the preflights after lunch. Right, I'm signing off. Everyone close up your stations and let's get to the briefings.'

Adam felt the aircraft rock slightly as people started to move. He did the same and, a minute or so later, they were all stood on the grass.

'Ah, good,' said Saunders, pointing. 'Here comes the refuelling bowser and a ground crew.'

'Hey, what the hell's going on?'

A furious looking officer had peddled up to them on his bicycle. It was Proudlove, the chief engineer.

They all saluted.

'Sir,' said Saunders. 'The machine – '

'Is it you that's taken my spare crew to work on this shit heap?'

'Well, yes but -'

'Didn't you hear? Harvey's put the kibosh on it, it's all off.'

'Oh,' said Saunders. 'I'm sorry, sir, I didn't know.'

'Well you bloody well do now,' said Proudlove. 'Now I've got to send all this lot back to where they should be. What a waste of...As you were.'

Proudlove threw his bike to one side and strode off towards the bowser.

Howard gave a deep sigh. 'Well thank God for that. Someone's seen sense.'

Although he didn't like the man, Adam couldn't help

but agree with him.

LMF 21

'The pilot and engineer carried out their inspection of the aircraft later than would normally have occurred, but it is not believed that this had any impact on the preparation of the aircraft.'

26/1/44/ 10.20 am

Douglas checked his watch again. The pilots' briefing would have started. He couldn't help that, he'd have to miss it for once, it was more important for him to be here.

At least it would be if the engineer, Harrison, turned up.

He had an idea who he was, an Aussie who had survived a mid-air collision over the airfield. Although a fellow sergeant, Douglas had never spoken with him but that wasn't too surprising, he wasn't one for mixing.

The outer door to the adjutant's office opened.

'- get you back as soon as we can, Harrison. Ah, here' s Dag. Dag, you know Harrison, don't you?'

'Not really -'

'Good, well I'm sure you two have a lot to do. I'll leave you to it.'

'Sir,' said both sergeants as the adjutant retreated behind his door again.

The two men stood awkwardly together. It was who Douglas thought it was, the scars on the man's head told their own story but so did Harrison'red-rimmed eyes. He was unshaven and stank of sweat, stale smoke and cheap whisky.

He obviously knew how he looked. 'I didn't expect to be flying,' he muttered. 'I've had some bad news.'

Great, thought Douglas, they've given me a lush.

'Well, you can smarten yourself up later. We've got an aircraft to check.'

'What about the -'

'Forget the briefings,' said Douglas. 'This is more important.'

'Yes sir,' said Harrison and he obediently followed Douglas outside.

They walked in silence over to C-Charlie. Douglas was pleased to see the fuel bowser by the aircraft but that was about it. There was little activity around it. If anything, the mechanics were packing up.

'What the hell? Come on, Harrison.'

Douglas broke into a run, not caring if the engineer was able to keep up with him.

'Hey, you!' he yelled at a private who was rolling up one of the bowser's hoses. 'What are you doing? You can't have fuelled it already?'

The man looked confused but saluted. 'Fuelled, sir? But...it's not flying.'

'Not flying? Of course it is. Damn well get it done, now!' He grabbed hold of the private and shoved him towards the bowser.

'You! Sergeant! What the bloody hell do you think you're doing?' A ground crew sergeant was bearing down on Douglas.

'What do you think I'm doing? I'm getting him to do his job - and yours too, you lazy bastard.'

The man loomed over Douglas. He was red in the face. 'Don't you speak to me like that. Just because you've got wings on your chest doesn't make you better than me.'

'Of course it does.'

'Why you little -'

Douglas was primed for the fight, his fists balled, he drew his arm back in preparation to start swinging - but then felt it grasped in a grip like iron.

'Skip,' said a quiet Aussie voice in his ear. 'We won't be flying anywhere if you're in the brig, mate.'

Douglas continued to bristle, the blood was pounding in his head, he wanted to punch someone.

At that moment a WAAF walked up. She looked puzzled, rather wary, but saluted and passed the maintenance sergeant the flimsy she was holding.

He looked at it and frowned, then sighed and turned away.

'Fuel it,' he said to the private. 'I'll go and get the rest of the boys back.'

LMF 22

26/1/44 11.30 am

R oland got an instant lift when he saw who was waiting outside the officers' mess.

'Excuse me, Flying Officer Saunders,' Connie
said, giving a crisp salute. 'Can we talk?'

'Of course, Warrant Officer Little,' he said, returning
the salute. 'Excuse me,' he said to Howard and Taylor who
were still with him.

He waited until they'd gone. 'What's wrong?'

'What do you think's wrong?' she said. A group of
WAAFs passed, chatting and laughing, offering casual salutes
in their approximate direction. 'Let's walk. I feel like we're in
a goldfish bowl here.'

They set off together, walking shoulder to shoulder,
Roland could feel her proximity, it was almost electric, a near
physical longing that was a pleasure and a torture at the same
time.

'I want to touch you,' he murmured. 'It seems odd not
to.'

'Well we can't so that's an end to it.'

The waspishness of her reply was a shock. What had
brought this on? Unless...

'You've seen Dag,' he said.

'Of course I've seen Dag.'

'Does he know?'

'Of course not!'

He took a deep breath. 'We've got to tell him.'

'We bloody well can't now, can we?' Connie did not normally swear so the word came almost as a slap. 'When were you going to tell me?'

'Tell you?' He was lost for a moment but then realised what she was talking about. 'Oh, the raid.'

'Yes, the raid, of course the raid! What possessed you? Flying with Dag of all people, today, on your first day back. I mean...why?'

'He...asked me. He needs one more to complete his tour. What else could I do?'

'Said no.'

'How? Come on, Connie, how could I refuse him?'

She stopped walking. 'Easily,' she said.

'On what grounds? I'm his friend, and he needed a navigator. It's what I do.'

'On what grounds?' She stared at him incredulous. 'He's cracking up. He's not stable, for God's sake! His own crew refused to fly with him any more. And secondly...well, you know the second reason why not.'

She was breathing heavily, clearly struggling with her emotions.

'We need to tell him,' he said again. 'It's not fair.'

'Of course we need to tell him! But we can't now can we? Not with you flying with him tonight. He's bad enough normally but -'

'But we're not flying. It's off. We haven't got an engineer.'

'Yes you have and you *are* flying. I was with Dag when he got the word.' She closed her eyes. 'It's not fair, it really isn't. I only just found you and now...'

Her voice trailed off.

'It's war, my love. It's what I do.'

'I just thought we'd have longer. It's too soon. I'm not ready.'

He took a step towards her, desire overcoming protocol, his hands reaching for her.

'Hey! Roland, what are you doing?'

Dag's shout made him jump.

'Dag...I...er...we...'

'Why aren't you at the briefings?'

'We were told it was off, sorry.'

'What, you mean no one's at them? Oh, for fuck's sake!'

'Calm down, Dag, I'll go and round them up. It's not too late, they'll get the end of it. Connie...we'll talk later.'

She just nodded.

Roland saw Dag look at her, then at him, and then back at Connie again.

He knows, he thought. Oh God, he knows.

LMF 23

26/1/44 11.40 am

'Your tea and teacake, sir.'

'Thank you, Edwards.' Howard frowned at the plate. 'Is that all the butter there is?'

'We're running a bit short, sir. I had to pinch some from the luncheon service.'

Howard sighed. 'Ah well, I suppose it will have to do.'

'Ah, Leslie, there you are, I've been looking for you.'

Howard looked up to find Saunders stood over him.

'Roly, old chap, pull up a pew,' he said.

'There isn't time. We're back on. You need to get over and catch the end of your briefing.'

'Oh come on, you can't be serious?'

'I am. Come on, please.'

'But I've just got...' He waved his hand at his plate.

'You'll have to leave it. I'm sorry.' Saunders looked at his watch. 'Hell. I need to get to *my* briefing. You are coming, aren't you?'

'Of course,' said Howard, rising. 'I just need to sign the chit.'

Saunders smiled. 'Good man.'

Once he had left, Howard sat down again. He stirred

two spoonfuls of sugar into his tea and buttered his teacake.

'I'd better get you that chit, sir,' said Edwards.

'There's no hurry. I'm not rushing my food for anyone. If they can't get themselves organised it's not my fault, is it?'

'Er, no, sir, I suppose not.' said Edwards. 'Will that be all, sir?'

'Yes - no, wait.'

'Yes sir?'

'Do you cover the sergeants' mess, Edwards?'

'Sometimes, sir, when they're short handed.'

'So you'll know some of the sergeant pilots?'

'Some of them, sir, yes.'

'Atkinson-Grieve?'

Howard could see that the man did. There was a tiny movement of his mouth, a twitch of the eyebrows.

'I...er...not really, sir,' said Edwards.

'Come on, man, you do, don't you? I can tell.'

'I don't gossip, sir. I don't want to speak out of turn.' Edwards looked uncomfortable.

'This is important,' Howard said. 'I order you to tell me what you know.'

Now the steward looked really uncomfortable. 'I don't know much, sir, I've only heard what others say. The gentleman doesn't come in the mess much and the others, well, they don't like him, they don't think he belongs. He's not one of theirs, see and -'

'Just tell me what you've heard and be quick about it.'

Edwards did just that, and then hurried off.

It was a long while before Howard remembered his tea

Malcolm Havard

and, by then, it was stone cold.

LMF 24

'All the crews assigned to the raid, including that of C-Charlie, rested during the afternoon of 26th January.'

26/1/44 1.30 pm

John lay on his bed trying to make himself sleep.

It was not going to happen, his mind was on fire, his thoughts racing.

So much had happened in the last few hours, he'd been swept along like he'd stepped into a river in flood. The current had snatched him away, taking him where it wanted to, tossing him this way and that. It was all too much, too quick, he didn't feel at all ready.

He certainly wasn't ready to sleep but if he didn't how was he going to be able to do his job tonight? What if he fell asleep? He could take Benzedrine, but his mum and dad wouldn't approve, no drugs, no alcohol. He might not have a choice though, everyone would be relying on him.

His mum and dad. He'd had a letter come from them, in response to news of his posting. His father had been business-like in it, his mother unusually emotional. It reminded him again that he was an only child, their only child, the centre of their world. If he died…no, no, he had to stop thinking like that.

His roommate and, now, crewmate had come back about twenty minutes ago and laid on his own bed. John still hadn't spoken to him, he couldn't think of anything to say, they had nothing in common. He didn't seem friendly to anyone but seemed to reserve, if not hostility, then at least a special cold indifference towards John.

The atmosphere in the room had changed as soon as Harrison had returned. It was no longer John's, he was just a guest now, an unwelcome one. He was afraid to move, apprehensive even about breathing less it caused offence.

Harrison's smell crept around him, a mix of oil, petroleum, cigarettes, sweat and spirits. It was like the engineer was reaching out to take full possession of his room.

LMF 25

26/1/44 1.36 pm

Burt lay, fully clothed, on the bed and stared at the ceiling. He didn't see it, did not see the grey, January, Cambridgeshire afternoon, he was lost in the pulsating, all encompassing heat of a New South Wales summer and its endless blue skies.

He also saw his wife, white with pain, racked with worry, gasping the last hours of her life away.

How long would it take him to get home? Two weeks? Three? Whatever, it would not be fast enough, she'd be long gone. He wouldn't see Mags again in this world, save in his thoughts and dreams.

He'd not treated her well. Yes, he'd always been faithful, he'd never messed around but that wasn't enough. He'd stayed at the pub late, night after night, whilst she'd been home with the kids, the kids who always seemed to have something, chicken pox, measles, colds. She had to scrimp and make do whilst he'd pissed his wages up the wall.

Sure, she hadn't borne it quietly, she'd always told him what she thought, strewth, hadn't she though? He was always getting the rough edge of her tongue, she'd threatened to leave a dozen times, but she'd always stayed and so had he. The passing years had, in fact, brought them closer. He'd changed, not much but enough for her to acknowledge the effort, albeit silently.

They'd had an understanding. Both knew the boundaries.

But then he had left. Not for another woman but because he'd been given a good excuse, to defend his country but it was an adventure, that was the truth, it was going to be a laugh.?

He never thought he'd end up in the old country. He never thought she'd get sick. He never thought of the kids. He never thought he might not come back.

Perhaps they'd put that on his tombstone: 'He never thought'.

Well he was thinking now, he couldn't do anything else. He'd checked over the machine in a daze, God knows whether he'd missed anything. Probably not, he'd done it so often he was sure he could do it in his sleep.

He heard his roommate roll over. He looked so much like his eldest lad, it hurt to even glance at him. Boys were fighting now, how long before Shane had to go?

He never thought it would come to this.

LMF 26

26/1/44 2.05 pm

After the previous night Roland needed to sleep but, of course, he couldn't.

His thoughts were, at first, of Connie, of where they had been twelve hours before, together in the hotel room. Pure pleasure, total guilt. They should have waited, they should have done the right thing by Dag, they'd agreed that, but all sense had gone driven away by the overwhelming, mutual need.

It hadn't been planned. She had been on leave, her home close to where he was recuperating. She had wanted to see him to talk about Dag, his temper and mood swings that made life with him near impossible. Roland had been having the usual pressures from home, they had helped each other, hared each other's problems.

Pressure from home. Roland closed his eyes and sighed.

He could picture his father, how he had looked when he visited the hospital. He barely asked how Roland was, his main aim clearly was to remind him that he was a Quaker and of the declaration the Quakers had made to Charles II, that 'We utterly deny all outward wars and strife and fighting with outward weapons for -'

'But, father,' he had said. 'The Nazi's oppress -'

'"- For *any* end, or under *any* pretence whatsoever. This is our testimony to the whole world." That is our belief.'

'Yes, father, I know,' he had said.

His father shook his head. 'You know this, yet still you have taken up arms.'

'I'm just a navigator, I just -'

'You navigate a weapon of war, don't you?'

'Yes.'

'I just don't understand how you can.'

He had stopped arguing out loud but did within. He knew he did it because it might be wrong, but it was also right too. Like being with Connie, wrong but oh-so right.

And both came with huge amounts of guilt.

LMF 27

D ouglas was too wired to sleep. Fortunately, his roommate wasn't, giving him the chance to chain smoke
cigarette after cigarette without complaints.

Tonight he'd complete his tour. Tonight it would be over.

Unless they scrubbed it.

No, no, surely, they wouldn't do that? He'd checked the weather, not great but not bad enough to scrub. It was going to happen.

The 6th of November. That was when he'd done mission 26. His crew had been sobbing, pleading, as they went around over the target and repeated the bombing run five times because the bomb aimer couldn't see the markers and he wouldn't let him just unload. That night he'd come to blows in the cockpit with the bloody idiot of a navigator who had replaced Roland, who'd come and ordered him to turn back.

He should have got a medal for that night, instead he got a reprimand. They'd covered it up, removed him from the crew, persuaded the navigator, an officer of course, not to press charges. He'd stayed on the squadron, kept his rank but been condemned to the drip drip Chinese water torture that was flying as a substitute pilot. A substitute with a reputation, the subject of whispers, rumours, mistrust.

Mission 27 came at the end of November, 28 on the

15th of December and then the 29th on the last day of the year.

Then nothing.

Nothing but waiting. Nothing but constant arguments and bickering with Connie, nothing but worries about his sanity.

Connie. She'd stopped understanding or, at least, trying to understand. That was another reason why getting to the end of his tour was important. He could relax then, surely that would give them a chance.

But was that true? That was another fear. Could he live without flying on ops? More than once he had found himself wishing that the war would go on forever. He didn't like killing but the risk, the life, it was so immediate, so vital. Something he couldn't live with but couldn't do without.

Like Connie.

She'd changed. She was different, so different from the woman he had fallen for last summer.

She was also different from the Connie who'd left on leave a week ago. Had something happened?

He thought of Connie. He thought of Roland. He thought of seeing them both together, the way they looked at each other.

No. Surely not. Roland was his friend. Connie wouldn't do that.

He lit another cigarette.

LMF 28

Gerry woke with a start.

It was very dark, had he overslept? He looked at the luminous dial of his watch, no, he was fine, it was just after three. He sank back down onto the bed, trying to relax. Given the circumstances, though, that was impossible.

He glanced across at his roommate. Was he asleep? It was hard to tell.

They used to be so close but now, whilst Adam was still his friend, he had become much more closed, more guarded since - well, since it had happened.

Since. Everything was since and before.

Before he had had friends, great, lovely friends with bonds that was close to love. In one case, it *was* love, though only in one direction - from him towards John.

John, of course it had to be A John, didn't it? He was beautiful, blonde, young. Gerry had been smitten from day one, barely able to talk to him. Things should have stayed that way, if only he hadn't got drunk, amorously tipsy, then none of this would have happened. The rejection, the binge that followed, the trouble he'd got into in Cambridge, Adam coming to the rescue but, in doing so, they'd both missed that night's flight.

The crew - their crew, their friends - had flown without them. They'd died without them. The loss was like losing a limb.

The loss had both saved and condemned him.

The authorities had taken pity, he'd got a reprimand for being drunk but that was all. He was condemned to living with what he had done and to seeing Adam's face day after day.

He couldn't ignore it, but he couldn't be sorry for himself. All he could do was be the best he could be, bury what he was and how he felt deep inside, and try to get through this.

Ignore new John's when they came along, however gorgeous they might be. Mourn, curse and hide, that was his present and future.

And to be hated by Adam.

LMF 29

26/1/44 3.06 pm

Adam lay awake.

He was never good at sleeping before raids, he survived on nervous energy that carried him through the night but, after touchdown, he barely reached the debrief before he started to nod. Getting to his bed, he'd sleep for ten hours at a stretch.

On non-raid nights he brooded too, thinking, worrying, he'd become acquainted with 2, 3 and 4am. As a result he was dog-tired, his mind dulled, stomach churning, his thoughts jumbled yet monotonous at the same time.

He thought of Sarah.

He thought of the baby, his unborn son or daughter.

That he wasn't going to see them. He wasn't coming back.

He looked over at the dark shape that was his room-mate. Gerry had saved them from their friends' fate, but he had also doomed them to the slow torture of waiting for their executioner, the chop that was sure to happen, probably tonight.

He should have been more careful on his leave, not let his desire take over. Then there would have been no baby - no, no, no! He wasn't wishing his first born out of existence, he wasn't wishing it harm.

It - her. He was looking into her eyes. Beautiful eyes.

Beautiful, blue, bright.

Bright points of light in the darkness, closing, closing.

They multiplied. Not eyes, what were they?

Shells. Cannon shells! Oh God, a fighter.

His guns wouldn't fire. He couldn't move, couldn't escape.

The perspex shattered. He screamed.

From across the room, Gerry said: 'Adam? What's wrong?'

LMF 30

26/1/44 4.01 pm

'Excuse me, David, can I have a quick word?'

Harvey looked up to find the squadron's MO stood in his doorway.

'What about, Doc?' he said. 'I've got the briefing in half an hour.'

'I know. I wouldn't bother you normally but -'

'But you're going to anyway.' Harvey sighed. 'Come on then, get it over with, but make it quick.'

The doctor stepped into the office and shut the door behind him. 'It's two things really, though they may be related. Pilot Officer Howard and Dag.'

Harvey raised his eyes to the heavens. 'Of course, I should have known. What is it now?'

'Well, I'll start with Howard. He came to me about half an hour ago claiming he couldn't fly because he had a gippy tummy.'

'Did he indeed?' said Harvey. 'Well, at least the windy windbag chose something appropriate. I hope you gave him what for.'

'I did. I gave him some milk of magnesia and told him that it would probably clear up. He'll probably come back though.'

'Probably. But what's the connection with Dag? Ah,

99

wait, of course, he's the bomb aimer that young Saunders recruited for tonight, isn't he?'

'Yes, he is.'

'So what do you think? That he's heard the whispers about our double-barrelled sergeant pilot and doesn't like the sound of them?'

'I think so.'

'But, of course, he's too bloody yellow to come to me and man up about it. Typical!' Harvey shook his head in exasperation. 'Well I'm not having it. Edith! Come in here.' His WAAF secretary opened the office door. 'Get Pilot Officer Howard over here, ASAP.'

'Yes, sir.'

Harvey turned to the doctor. 'You're still here,' he said.

'There's Dag.'

'I thought we'd dealt with that?'

'No, this is something else. I've had people keeping an eye on him, just quietly, and my spies tell me that the stress is showing again. He came close to laying someone out this morning.'

'Who? An officer? If it was, I want to know.'

The MO shook his head. 'No, it was a senior NCO. I won't say who because he doesn't want to take it further -'

'I wish he did. I'd have Dag on a charge then. That would get rid of him. But that's not going to happen is it? So why tell me?'

'I just wondered, given what happened, whether it was wise to let him fly tonight. His level of instability -'

'Level of instability? For God's sake, we're fighting a war here. Everyone needs to be a bit loopy to do what we do. Why should I make him a special case?'

The MO stared at him 'Because of the crew?'

'As I said before, none of them are going to be a major loss to us.' There was a knock on the door. 'Yes?'

The WAAF opened it and stepped inside.

'I've got Pilot Officer Howard, sir.'

'Show him in - Doc, you can stay. Ah, Howard, close the door.'

'Sir.' Harvey saw Howard glance nervously at the Doctor. Good, he thought, he's guessed. Time to lay it on thick.

'Howard, you are, in my opinion, a piece of shit, a total waste of time. God only knows how you passed out as qualified because you're totally useless. Now the Doc here tells me you're pretending to be sick to get out of tonight's mission. Well, we're not having it, y'hear? You'll fly tonight and you'll do a decent job or else, tomorrow, you'll be in the brig and then you'll be out of here with LMF plastered all over your file and your rank insignia torn off. Now get out of my sight.'

Pale faced and trembling, Howard saluted and left.

LMF 31

'The final target briefing went ahead as normal at 1630 hours. No specific issues with the target or its defences were identified.'

26/1/44 4.35pm

The feeling that John was being carried headlong into something he wasn't ready for was especially strong in the briefing.

The room was like a theatre, the audience rowdy, excited but wary at the same time, waiting for the show to start. It was filled with noise, laughter, high-pitched voices, brittle, strained,but full of bravado. It was also filled with a thick fug, most of the men were smoking. John, who didn't, found his head thumping, though he was not certain whether this was due to the lack of fresh air or because of his racing heart.

It would not sink in; this was real, *he* was a part of this, part of the squadron, part of the war effort, part of the crew. Yes, these men around him were *his* crew. His life was in their hands and theirs were in his, he was their link to the outside world, he would record and relay instructions from base and the Master Bomber.

Quietly, before the briefing party came in, he took a quick, appraising look at his companions, his crew.

He didn't know them. There hadn't been time. But then how much did you actually get to know someone, really know them, even when you had known them for years? He had, at least formed some impressions over the course of the day. Saunders, for example, it was obvious he was a nice chap, steady, patient, helpful, a reassuring presence.

How about the rest though?

The gunners he didn't know as well. Pascoe - Gerry, he had to call him Gerry - he seemed friendly enough, very friendly in fact. Taylor though was different, distant, aloof to the point of coldness. There seemed to be some issue between him and Gerry, Taylor had been short and snappy with him a couple of times, seemingly without noticing he'd done it. Gerry had laughed it off, but John was sure he'd been hurt. Both seemed decent enough types though.

How about the others? He was less sure about them. His parents had always told him not to judge a book by its cover, but it was hard not to.

His own roommate, Harrison. He still hadn't really talked to him. He'd looked shocked when he'd found that John was in the crew though John had no idea why he'd upset him. The man looked terrible, he bore scars on his body, but he clearly had deeper ones within. He was ill kempt, dishevelled, though he now, at least, had had a wash but John suspected that this was more down to the need to cover the whisky fumes than anything else. Did he pay the same amount of attention to his job? John had to hope that he was more diligent in that area.

Howard, the bomb aimer, he wasn't at all sure about him. He was the only one of the officers who really let John know he was always inferior in rank and that this had to be respected . Something, though, had changed during the day. The bluster had gone, he'd come into the briefing white-faced and quiet. He had not spoken to anyone, had not made eye contact with anyone. Even now he was staring at the floor in front of him.

The contrast with the demeanor of their skipper was marked. Dag, as everyone seemed to call him, was a bundle of nervous energy, unable to sit still. His feet were constantly moving, tapping, shifting like a dancer forced to sit out a foxtrot. He fiddled with his hands, scratching, running his fingers through his hair, checking his watch every few seconds.

He'd heard that pilots were selected for bombers rather than fighters because of their steadiness, their ability to work within and bond a team. How did Dag fit into that?

He had to stop thinking like that, he was being unfair.

John's reverie was ended by the arrival of the briefing party. There was a scraping of chairs, a mass stubbing out of cigarettes as the CO, the meteorologist and the intelligence officers swept in, walking confidently down the aisle.

Harvey mounted the stage and strode to the front, facing the audience, stood with legs apart, hands behind his back, next to the still shrouded blackboard. He waited for a moment for the room to fall quiet.

It did.

'Gentlemen,' he said. 'Please be seated.'

He now had his hand on the sheet covering the blackboard. John found he was holding his breath, he was sure he was not alone.

'The target for tonight is...' Harvey said, and pulled the sheet off the board. '...Essen.'

There was a collective sigh and groan.

LMF 32

'As C-Charlie was a late addition to the squadron roll it was allocated the final take-off slot.'

26/1/44 5.15 pm

'So, gentlemen, first take-off is at twenty-oh-five with the last machine away at twenty-one-ten. Do the squadron proud, do me proud. And good luck.'

'Cheers, we'll bloody well need it,' someone near to Adam muttered. Whoever it was did not seek to keep his voice down and Adam saw Harvey scan the audience for the culprit.

'Bloody Happy Valley again,' said someone else. 'Who's upset Butch?'

The new man, Hiley, was looking nervous. 'Don't worry,' he murmured to him. 'As long as we all do our jobs, we'll be fine.'

Although his words sounded hollow and insincere even to himself, the radio operator did at least, nod and smile.

'Right, everyone, listen up.' Dag waited for them to gather round him. 'We're last off, we're going to be tail-end Charlie, I'm afraid.'

'Oh, it just gets better and better, doesn't it?' said Howard.

Dag glared at him. 'We couldn't expect anything else. We're a late addition.'

'Late and ill-considered,' said Howard. 'Sacrificial lambs. The defence will be ready for us. We're stuffed.'

'That's enough of that,' said Dag. 'Don't put the new chap off, we'll be fine. Just get on with your job.'

Adam winced. This was just the wrong thing to say to the blustering Howard.

'Who the hell do you think you're talking to? Remember I'm an officer and you're just a bloody sergeant.'

'And you're bloody useless,' said Dag, stepping towards Howard and getting in his face. 'I'm your fucking skipper, don't you bloody forget that.'

Saunders put a hand on pilot's shoulder. 'C'mon, Dag, there's no need for this,' he said.

'If I say there's a need -'

'Dag, come on, let's get something to eat.'

Saunders was firmer now, he grabbed hold of Dag's arm and tried to tug him away. At first, Adam thought he was going to resist, might even lash out but, after a few more seconds of eyeballing Howard, he allowed himself to be led towards the door.

But then, abruptly, he turned back.

'Did everyone make their departmental briefings?' he said.

'Yes,' said Adam.

Everyone except Howard nodded.

Dag stared at him.

'You didn't, did you?' he said. 'Why not for fuck's sake? You fucking useless sod.'

'Of course I bloody well went, you guttersnipe.'

Adam was sure Howard was lying, Dag clearly felt the

same. He pointed at him.

'You bloody well better had done.'

'Or what, sergeant, or what?'

Dag stepped forward again, fists balled. This time Saunders was even rougher, grabbing hold of him in a bear-hug.

'Enough, Dag. He's not worth it. Don't get yourself locked up over him. Come on, now!'

Dag shrugged himself free. 'Yeah, yeah,' he said, turning on Saunders. 'We all have to be friends, don't we? That's you isn't it, hiding in your little map room whilst everyone else does the dirty work? It salves your conscience, doesn't it? I see that hasn't stopped you from -'

Abruptly, Dag turned away and walked out of the briefing room.

Adam noticed that Saunders had flushed red. He wondered what Dag was talking about, clearly the navigator knew.

Saunders gave a weak smile. 'Don't worry, chaps,' he said. 'Dag will calm down. See you all at dispersal. Oh, and Howard?'

'Yes?'

'Get the briefing notes off someone.'

'But -'

'Just do it.'

Saunders walked out of the room, followed, moments later, by Hiley and Howard.

He looked at Gerry. He looked like Adam felt, looked like he wanted to say what was foremost in Adam's mind.

Adam said it anyway.

'How the hell did we get involved in all this?'

LMF 33

'On completion of the briefing, an evening meal for the crews was served as normal in both the officers' and sergeants' messes.'

26/1/44 6.05 pm

'**M**ore tea, sir?'

Gerry looked up into the WAAF's eyes. He'd seen her before, he was sure, but couldn't place her. Oh yes, she'd served him at lunchtime. What was her name?

'Thanks, er...'

She smiled and shook her head. 'Mavis, sir. Oh dear, am I that forgettable?' She carefully topped up Gerry's cup from her teapot.

'Sorry, not at all, Mavis. I've just got a lot on my mind.'

She nodded and put her free hand on his shoulder and gave it at squeeze. 'Don't worry about it, everyone's uptight about the raid.' He expected - wanted - her to remove her hand but she kept it there. 'You will come back, won't you?' she added, more quietly.

Her touch was more than unwelcome, it almost made his flesh creep. He had to resist the temptation to shrug it off.

'I'll do my best,' he said.

'You do that,' she said. 'I'll be waiting up for you, how does that sound?'

'Wonderful,' said Gerry, with very little enthusiasm.

Still she kept her hand there for a few moments longer.

'Hey, Mavis, are you coming with that tea?' someone called from further down the table. 'I'm parched here!'

'Coming. Hold your horses,' she said and then, to Gerry's relief, was gone.

He found himself staring at the cup she had just filled. There was something revolting about the mix of colours that he'd never really noticed before, the green glaze to the pottery, its shade close to that of the paint applied to the inside of the fuselage of every aircraft he'd ever flown in, the orange/white melange of the liquid within, a slick of fat floating on top. His stomach churned, he didn't want it. Quickly he pushed it away.

'You shouldn't string her along like that,' Adam, sat alongside him, murmured. 'It's not fair on her.'

'It's her not me,' said Gerry. 'What am I supposed to do about it? What do I know about talking to women?'

'You've got a mother and a sister, haven't you? Anyway, you can learn. Like I said, it's not fair on her thinking she's got a chance.'

'Maybe she has,' said Gerry. 'It would solve a problem.'

Adam put down his knife and fork and turned to stare at him. 'No it wouldn't,' he said. 'You know it wouldn't.'

Gerry did not reply. He knew Adam was right, indeed, he didn't know why he'd said it, other than he had spent many sleepless hours thinking of ways of trying to conform, to keep his family's approval, to keep himself safe from his own urges and instincts. What good had those urges done for him? They'd already cost him his second family, his crew.

'So, what do we do?'

It took a few moments for Gerry to realise Adam had asked a question.

109

'Do about what?'

'About this mess we've got ourselves into, of course!' Adam's irritation was not disguised in any way. 'I don't trust the pilot or the engineer. We all know about Howard, he's a waste of space. Having any one of those would be enough but we've got all three and, to cap it all, the aircraft's a flying coffin.'

'Don't say that.'

'Well it's true. This game's dangerous enough as it is but this trip is looking like suicide.'

Gerry let Adam's words sink in, trying to find a counter argument. He couldn't.

'So what *do* we do?' he said at last.

Adam was silent for a long few seconds. When he spoke it was in a voice that was barely audible.

'They can't fly without gunners. They wouldn't find replacements in time,' he said.

'But we can't do that!' said Gerry. 'They'd throw the book at us.'

'We can't,' Adam muttered, then stared at Gerry.

Gerry looked back at his friend - or the man he'd always counted as his friend - in disbelief. This was his payback was it?

Then the disbelief turned to anger. 'I'm not doing that,' he said. 'We'll fly.'

And then he got up from the table and walked away.

LMF 34

26/1/44 8.30 pm

T he ground trembled as the black giant trundled past, the four Merlins at mid-throttle, propellers already on coarse pitch ready to bite into the air hauling tonnes of metal, perspex, explosives and blood, bone and flesh up into the atmosphere. As it passed there was a white blur by the left-hand side of the cockpit, the pilot waving. Automatically, Roland waved back.

Who was it? The markings were not clear. He tried to remember the take-off times, yes, that would be Watkins, the previous 'owner' of C-Charlie. He was in his new machine, the one that had just arrived from the depot. Roland felt like they were the poor relations, younger siblings putting up with hand-me-downs.

They'd only had one minor victory. Watkins wanted his new mount to become C-Charlie, in fact he'd got het up about it when he'd been told that there wasn't time to do the repaint. Roland understood all too well why; superstition. C-Charlie had been lucky for them, to fly under another name was disturbing but, under sufferance, he and his crew had accepted that, for tonight at least, they were in Z-Zulu.

He turned his back on Watkins' machine as it turned onto the taxiway. As a final insult, the four props flung water from the damp concrete over the crew waiting to board their own machine.

He'd never departed from a mission so close to the

admin block but, of course, C-Charlie had been effectively dumped there ready for disposal. At least they didn't have far to go.

It also meant that he was near Connie who was on duty in the radio room. He wondered whether she would take a moment to leave her post to watch them go. He looked across at the building, not seriously expecting to see anyone.

There was a shape - he couldn't see who, it was too far and too dark - stood in the doorway.

He checked the time, they'd be boarding soon. There was no time to find out who it was. Yet he had to.

'I won't be a moment,' he said, not even checking to see who he was stood next to, though he had a vague idea it was young Hiley, and set off towards the figure.

It was her.

'Aren't you on duty?' he said when he reached her.

'Yes, but they're covering for me,' she replied. 'I needed to...well, I needed to see you off.'

They stood together for a few awkward moments, then she stepped forward and put her arms around him, pressing herself against him.

'Connie.' he whispered. 'What if someone -'

'Let them,' she said. 'I don't care.'

Still he resisted holding her too. 'What about Dag?' he said.

'It's dark. He won't be able to see. Anyway, he'll know soon enough. Please, just hold me. I need it.'

He still hesitated, but then did as he was asked. It did feel wonderful, perfect. What they were doing had to be right.

Vaguely, in the distance, he heard the throttles open on the next machine to take off. That would be Watkins in Z-

Zulu, starting to roll. He could visualise it, waddling heavily, slowly accelerating, full of fuel and bombs. He would have to go, it would be their turn very soon.

The engine note changed. Someone yelled.

There was a thump, a flash of light, heat.

The airfield was suddenly bathed in a devilish, red glare as hundreds of incendiaries and thousands of gallons of aviation fuel burst out, tumbled and rolled down the grass beside the runway.

And amidst the horror of the sudden, violent death and immolation of Watkins and his crew, Roland saw something else, something that chilled him.

He could see his crew quite clearly - John, Taylor, Pascoe, Howard...and the engineer and Dag stood slightly apart from the rest under the port wing.

And Dag was not looking at the crash, but straight at him and Connie.

LMF 35

'As embarkation took place, it was discovered that C-Charlie had developed a minor technical fault.'

26/1/44 8.46 pm

B urt could not look at the burning wreckage, he had to turn away. It brought back too many memories.

The skipper wasn't looking either, he was staring in the opposite direction. They were stood together under the wing of their Halifax, sheltering from the light drizzle. The weather had changed during the day, becoming cloudy, warmer but, in doing so, had made the conditions more miserable.

He needed something to occupy his thoughts, away from Mags, away from burning aircraft. The ruddy glow from where Z-Zulu was burning at least allowed him to do a final, cursory check of C-Charlie. Everything looked fine, and he found himself staring at the water dripping off the trailing edge of the wing and the airframe.

There was something odd about them.

Some of the drips off the port outer engine looked... different. Or did they? Yes, they were dropping more slowly, like they were sticky, viscous. He took a few steps closer and then, when he was sure he wasn't imagining things, stood directly under the nacelle.

Now he could smell it as well as see it. Engine oil. Even in the dying illumination from the funeral pyre he could see a dark stain on the grass beneath.

'Oh fuck, fuck!' he muttered. 'Hey, you!' he called over to a group of mechanics watching Z-Zulu. 'Get some light over here.'

'Can't do that, sir. Chiefy won't like it, not with the blackout.'

'What blackout?' Burt yelled, pointing at the burning wreckage. 'Get over here and bring a torch with you.'

A couple came over, one fiddling with a flashlight.

'Give that here.' Burt grabbed it and shone the light over the sides of the engine. He couldn't believe what he saw. The engine was dripping oil, the bottom was covered in it. 'Strewth!How the fuck? Oh bleedin', blindin' bloody hell! Where's it coming from?'

'Oil line, probably,' said one of the mechanics. 'Must be split or summat.'

'Nah, it'll be the tank. Seam must have gone.'

'Jesus, it's some leak though.'

'Stop stating the bleeding obvious. Go and get the chief - now!'

One of the men ran off towards the hangar. Burt looked again at the engine and then across at the skipper. He was neither looking at Z-Zulu nor seemed to have noticed the commotion not twenty feet away from him. He looked to be in a world of his own.

Well, he was going to have to know. Burt swallowed. He was not looking forward to this.

'Er, Skip, we've got a problem.'

He was expecting an explosion.

He was not wrong.

LMF 36

26/1/44 8.54 pm

'**H**ow did you miss it? How? How?'

John could only hear one side of the conversation. He was still with Howard and the two gunners a little way away from where the mechanics, pilot, engineer and Saunders were, near the port outer.

Saunders put his hand on Dag's shoulder. The pilot angrily shrugged it off.

'Don't talk rot, leave me alone!'

'What an angry, pathetic little man he is,' murmured Howard.

'Leave it out, Leslie,' said Taylor. 'Don't make it worse.'

'How can I make it worse?'

'Believe me, carry on the way you are, and you'll find out.'

'From that common little nonentity? I think not.'

'Have it your own way, Leslie.'

John glanced across at the three officers, their faces ruddy and satanic from the fire and tried to make sense of the last twenty minutes.

The tension had built as each of the squadron's aircraft

had started up, taxied round to the end of the runway, revved up the engines and then lumbered into the air because he knew it was soon to be their turn. They had just about to board, he had taken one last look at the runway, at the black shadow that was gathering speed.

At first he could not work out what was happening, the shape seemed to grow vertically, was it a trick of the light?

Then his brain resolved what he was seeing. It was a Halifax, in plan view, like he was looking down at it, one wing reaching high up into the sky as if it were grasping at the overcast whilst the other was digging into the ground. Then, in an orange flash, the picture splintered, tearing itself apart. Fireflies of incendiaries raced ahead of a blooming, rolling fire of high-octane fuel as the liquid explosives burst from the tanks.

It was terrifying, yet oddly beautiful.

It was also imprinted on John's mind. He was still shaking.

'Are you all right, John?'

He looked into the smiling face of Pascoe.

'Yes sir, I'm fine.'

'Forget the sir. It's Gerry.'

'Thanks Gerry.' He looked across at the pilot and mechanics. 'Will we be...?'

'Going? I don't think so. Not now anyway. The machine's U/S and there's no spare.'

'Oh, right.'

'Don't look so disappointed, boy,' said Howard. 'This has probably saved all our lives. Ill thought through, wrong personnel, wrong pilot - don't look at me like that, Taylor, I'm just saying what we're all thinking.'

'We may be thinking it, but we don't say it,' Taylor muttered. 'Something's happening. What is it, Skip? What's going on?'

'Clear out of the way, you lot,' said Dag. 'We're going to tow the crate into the hangar.'

'What?' said Howard. 'You're going to try and repair it?'

'Of course we are! Now shift!'

'But...it's too late. And...it's fueled and bombed up. This is against regulations.'

Howard's bluster was ignored. A tug was driving towards C-Charlie, reversing to the tail to hook on and drag it away like a naughty child.

And, on the runway, after the shortest of breaks to allow the wreckage of Z-Zulu to be cleared off the runway, another Halifax started its take-off run.

John shook his head. Men had died and it did not seem to matter. How could that be right?

LMF 37

R oland found that he was stood on his own between the rest of the crew and those working on C-Charlie. That seemed appropriate, it about summed up where he was, connected but apart.

He always had been, his beliefs, his faith, had always made him different, but now his actions had distanced him from both his family and his fellow Quakers.

He was in between.

He had developed one good friend in the squadron, Dag. But now he and Connie had ended that. And now he was caught between those who were desperate to go and those who clearly preferred not to.

Dag was on edge, dangerously so, bouncing on the balls of his feet, checking his watch, pacing to and fro, unable to keep still. Harrison and the mechanics were working on the gantry above him, the inspection panels had been stripped off the engine and there was a growing pile of rags beneath them as they soaked up the oil, searching for the source of the leak. It looked hopeless, even if they found it would there be time for a repair?

Dag clearly thought the same.

'Come on, come on, have you found it yet?' he shouted up.

'Getting closer, Skip,' said Harrison, his hands and face

119

covered with the oil.

'Get on with it! We're running out of time.'

Roland would normally have gone over, tried to calm him down but, tonight, didn't think his intervention would help. Not after Dag had seen him and Connie together. What a stupid thing to have done, all their intentions of breaking it gently destroyed in a moment.

Well, it looked like they weren't going to fly together tonight. That was probably a blessing.

He glanced at the rest of the crew hovering by the door to the hangar, mugs of tea in hand, looking both conspicuous in their flying gear and a little lost.

Outside the giant folding doors, closed to stop the light spilling out, the airfield had gone quiet, the last aircraft having already taken off. Everyone had gone to the party except for them.

Was he relieved? Or would he have preferred to go and get it over with? He would have to go back on ops sometime so why not now?

It would certainly be best for Dag to go. He'd clearly got worse whilst Roland was away. His nerves were stretched as tight as a drum, he needed a rest before he broke, no wonder he was so desperate to fly this last mission.

Now it looked certain it wouldn't happen.

Roland would face being with him even longer. That wasn't going to be easy.

He suddenly didn't want to be between any more. He had to make a choice. He chose the rest of the crew.

'Chaps,' he said. 'How are you all doing?'

'How do you think we're doing?' said Howard. 'How long is this farce going to go on before that idiot faces facts? It's over, we're not going tonight.'

'We need to give them a chance to fix it,' said Roland, even though, for once, Howard's thinking was clearly in line with his own.

'Fix it? They've got no chance. Even if they do, how long is it going to take to get it back together again? Everyone's gone, in case you hadn't noticed. I vote we chuck it, go and turn in.'

'He's got a point,' said Taylor. 'Surely, we should scrub it, Roland?'

Roland looked across at Dag who was pacing like a caged lion beneath C-Charlie.

'All right,' he said at last. 'I'll go and have a word. Stay here for the time being, let's not give him a fait accompli - yes?'

'If we must,' sighed Howard.

Roland took a deep breath, gathered himself and made his way towards Dag.

LMF 38

Douglas saw Roland coming over. He quickly turned and hurried away.

He didn't want to talk to the bastard, it was all too much, not tonight. When were they going to tell him? How long had it been going on; how did he not see? He wanted to know - but, also, he didn't, not now anyway. He didn't have enough energy left.

He stared up at the men working on C-Charlie. In truth, he'd given up hope that there'd be a solution.

'What if we bind the pipe?'

'What, lag it?'

'Yes.'

'It's under pressure. It'd still leak.'

'Yeah, but not as badly.'

'Dag, can I have a word?'

It was Roland. He ignored him.

'Dag!'

'What the hell do you want?' he said, not looking.

'I've been talking to the chaps. They think we should scrub it. We've missed the boat.'

'Sod that, sod them and sod you. We haven't, not yet.'

He stepped forward. 'Harrison! Harrison! Have you found it?'

The engineer leaned away from the engine. 'Yes, Skip,' he said. 'It's a cracked pipe, close up to the tank.'

'Is it repairable?'

One of the other mechanics shook his head. 'It needs to be replaced, sir,' he said.

'How long will that take?'

'A couple of hours, sir.'

'Hours? Fuck that. Harrison, what was that you were talking about before, about binding it?'

The Australian pulled a face. 'I dunno, sir. It might not be a good idea.'

'Tell me.'

'I just thought if we put a sleeve of light grade aluminium round it, then bound it tightly with some hessian, well, I think it'd hold.'

'It'll leak,' said the mechanic. 'Bound to.'

'Not as badly,' said Harrison. 'And if we brim the tank...'

'How long?'

'Fifteen, twenty minutes.'

'Do it. Do it now, and be quick about it,' said Douglas.

'Sir, I can't...' said the mechanic.

'Just damn well get it done!' Now Douglas felt he could face Roland. 'Go and tell the crew we're flying.'

Roland looked aghast.

'But...we're late enough now. We could end up on our own over the target.'

'So? Someone has to be last. Go and get them ready.'

Still Roland hesitated. 'I think they've had enough,

Dag,' he said. 'I don't think...'

Douglas grabbed hold of his flying jacket. 'You don't think? You don't think what, Roland? You don't think I didn't know about you and Connie?' Roland tried to twist away but Douglas pulled him close, their faces close together. 'I thought you were my friend. I thought she was...Well, whatever, frankly, I don't care anymore. I just want to get done and get away from this place. Out of all your lives. I want to fly, and I want to do it tonight.' His voice softened. 'Once we get up, it'll be fine. It will. Please, do this for me.'

Roland stared at him for a moment, then nodded. He looked across at the rest of the crew.

'I'll do my best,' he said.

LMF 39

'Despite the delay caused by the technical issue, the crew were happy to fly on the mission.'

26/1/44 9.55 pm

'**B**ut this is ridiculous. Every other aircraft has gone - long gone, in fact.'

Roland felt his heart sink, even though it had been obvious that this would be the main argument against them going, he was hoping that they wouldn't use it quite so vehemently.

'Yes, they have,' he said. 'But, as we were the last in the stream anyway, it surely doesn't make a lot of difference.'

'Of course it does, you're talking utter rot.' Howard was warming to his task now. 'We'll end up alone over the target, all of the defences focused on us. It would be suicide.'

Roland knew that the bomb aimer's words were hitting home - and he was only saying what he, himself, was thinking.

'Actually that's not necessarily true.'

Pascoe's interruption came as a surprise.

'Of course it's true!' said Howard.

'No, it's not,' Pascoe said firmly. 'Adam and I ended up on our own over Frankfurt, late last year and that was one of the easiest trips we had. It was like Jerry couldn't be bothered with us.'

Roland saw Taylor glare at his colleague. Quickly though, before there was chance for anyone to counter, he moved to reinforce the advantage.

'You see? And that's not the first time I've heard that. I've known other skippers who preferred to go over the target later because the flak gunners were tired and their gun barrels red hot. The fire's less intense and less accurate.'

'And the nightfighters will have followed the rest of the stream.'

Pascoe was proving to be an unexpected ally.

'Or will be down refuelling and re-arming,' Roland added.

Howard sighed. 'That may be so but...'

'But what?'

'Well, how do we know that the crate's been repaired properly?' He pointed at C-Charlie. 'They're rushing if you ask me.'

'That's not fair, Howard. You know how good our chaps are, they're the best. They wouldn't let us fly if they weren't sure.'

Liar, he thought to himself. You bloody bare-faced liar.

'Look, all of you,' he said. 'I was over there when they found the fault. They gave me a guarantee that work will have been done properly. Don't forget I'm going to be flying too, as will Dag and Harrison. Do you think we'd be doing that if we thought the machine was u/s?'

Howard scowled at Dag. 'He's mad enough,' he said.

'Dag's not mad. He's brave and a superb pilot. I know, I flew a dozen missions with him before I got injured.'

Howard didn't stop frowning. He turned to the others. 'You, Taylor. You've been quiet. What do you think?'

'Probably the same as you,' said the gunner. 'But...if we refuse to go, would that mean we'd get disciplined? I wouldn't want to get branded LMF.'

'Surely it wouldn't come to that,' said Howard.

'It might,' said Taylor.

There was a long silence. Roland looked at each of the men in turn. There was one who hadn't yet spoken.

'John,' he said. 'Feel free to speak up. You've got a say too.'

The young wireless operator looked nervously at the others.

'Well, I don't know, sir,' he said. 'I've not flown before and -'

'Exactly!' said Howard. 'What does he know?'

'You've still got an opinion, John,' said Roland. 'One we'd like to hear, yes?'

Taylor and Pascoe, at least, nodded.

'Well, I suppose...' John began. 'Well, what I was thinking, this was what we train for, isn't it? This is what we do. Nothing about what we do is safe, it never can be. I...*we* - signed up to do this. I can't say I'm not scared because I am. But I'll still be scared tomorrow, or next week or next month or whenever we get to fly over Germany. Personally, I'd rather go and get it done, now, tonight. The sooner we do this the sooner it will be all over.'

John had been staring at the concrete floor as he spoke but now he looked up and seemed to remember where he was and the company he was in. 'Sorry, sirs, that's just how I was thinking. I'm sure you all know better than I do.'

127

LMF 40

'C-Charlie took off at around 2200 and climbed out over the North Sea following the rest of the bomber stream.'

26/1/44 10.18 pm

Douglas raced C-Charlie down the taxiway, pushing much faster than he normally would have. He kept one eye on the control tower, expecting the recall signal. After everything else today it seemed inevitable.

Why was he bothering? He'd lost Connie, what was the point? Everything he'd done, all that he'd focussed on was aimed at getting this trip done. Once he had, everything would change, he could relax, be a different person - perhaps the man he was before.

But who was that man? Could he remember? It was someone he was hoping to rediscover, to relax into, and then she and him...

But there was no she and him because they'd betrayed him.

How could they? The woman he'd adored, who'd loved him as he was, who'd saved him from himself and his best friend, possibly his only friend on the squadron, one of the few people here he liked. How could they do this to him?

Perhaps it was all a lie, it was all fake, always had been.

So, there was his answer, why he was doing this, so he could get away, get it done and get out of here, as far as possible from the pair of them.

He stared at the control tower. Don't do it. Don't stop us. Let me go.

C-Charlie bumped, bounced, rocked. He'd strayed off the taxiway.

'Easy, Skip, not so fast.'

'Shut it, Burt, I know what I'm doing.'

But he did ease the throttle back, his gaze never leaving the control tower.

LMF 41

R oland had been tossed sideways by the bump. As he pushed himself upright, he saw the pale faces of the rest of the crew, clustered in the centre of the aircraft for take-off, just in front of the main spar, this was the strongest and safest part of the machine.

This would have been the picture in every Halifax flying tonight, including that of Z-Zulu. What would it have been like for Watkins and his crew? They would have had a few moments knowing something had gone wrong, terror as they were flung around and then hurled into the hereafter.

It was a horrible thought, one he wished he hadn't had, but, of course, he couldn't unthink it now.

He wasn't ready for this, he'd been thrown back into this world, it had happened so fast, he hadn't prepared himself.

Twenty-four hours ago, where had he been? He knew exactly where; with Connie, making love, enveloped in passion as much as he was physically enveloped in her.

They'd had a plan, a strategy to ease the impact on Dag, but it had been swept away, first by Roland being declared fit and posted back, then by their irresistable physical needs, and, finally, by being caught up in the rush to fly this mission.

It was all too soon, everything was happening too fast, he wasn't ready.

But he had no choice.

John was sat at his radio station. Even in the darkness Roland could see that he was gripping the table hard. What was it like for him? He'd had no time to settle in, he'd been dropped into it, it was even less fair on him.

'Don't worry, John,' he called. 'We'll soon be off and then we'll be fine.'

John didn't reply, though, in the darkness, Roland thought he saw his head nod in acknowledgement.

He was going through the motions of politeness because, Roland guessed, he didn't believe it either.

LMF 42

'Flaps 35.'

Burt already had his hands on the flap controls. He pulled it down to the correct setting.

'Flaps for take-off, Skip.'

'Radiators shut. Air intakes cold.'

'Check, Skip.'

He felt Dag open the throttles, holding the machine on the brakes for a couple of seconds, then ease them closed again. Good, the Skip was in a rush, but he was doing things right.

'Brakes off - throttle.'

C- Charlie started to roll, Burt's hand covering Dag's as he slowly advanced the four throttle levers to their full power. He scanned the instruments, checking the revs, the oil pressure, the phosphorescent telltales all level. He looked at all four but paid special attention to the port outer. It should be fine, the bodge should hold.

It should be right.

Be right.

The aircraft shuddered, rocked, the power coursing through every rivet. It was, suddenly, a vibrating, quivering, eager beast, desperate to join the rest of its pack, far ahead in the night sky.

I'm coming back to you, Mags, he thought, I've set off.

The familiar feelings came back, driving away memories of the horror and the panicked rush of the last hour. He'd done this twenty-two times before, mostly with his crew, his mates.

His mates.

He was back in F-Freddie again, his pilot, Alex, alongside him, solid, dependable.

Until the red flash of fire, the splintering of perspex, the shock of the night air slapping his face like an open palm, the sinking, tumbling, falling.

'Brakes. Gear up.'

Shaking, tumbling, falling into the darkness.

'Brakes! Gear up, gear up!'

Burt came back into the moment. Not Alex, that was Dag. This was C-Charlie, not Freddie.

'Sorry, Skip,' he said, applying the brakes to stop the wheels rotating then selecting the lever to bring the gear up.

The feeling of sinking lessened, C-Charlie had started to gain airspeed and height now the drag had reduced.

That was close. What the hell had just happened there? Nothing, he told himself, he was just tired. Today had been rough but, still, this wouldn't do. He needed to be on his game, do his job.

He was okay, he was fine.

But his hands were shaking as they rested on the flap controls.

LMF 43

26/1/44 10.22 pm

John was shaking.

In fact he was shaking so hard that he had to grip the edges of his radio table to try and control himself.

This was stupid, he'd flown at night before, in Halifaxes. What made this different?

It was different because that was training, this was the real thing. He couldn't kid himself that it was anything other, it was happening.

He also couldn't get the image of Z-Zulu's violent end out of his mind.

He couldn't do this, he couldn't, he was going to freeze, he was going to let them all down. He had struggled to get his food down in the canteen two hours ago but now he wished he hadn't. The bile was rising into his mouth.

He couldn't be sick. He couldn't fail, these men were relying on him. He had to do what he'd been trained to.

He couldn't let mother and father down. He was all they had, there was just him.

He'd make them proud. He had to be a man. It was what was expected of him.

John forced the acid back down and adjusted his headphones.

LMF 44

'C-Charlie climbed to its allocated altitude and followed the same route as the other bombers in the stream.'

26/1/44 10.28 pm

'**R**ight, it's time.'

Gerry pressed his mouth close to Adam's ear to be heard over the roaring engines, the vibration and rushing noise of the air being battered out of the path of the airframe. Even through the aromas filling the machine - petrol, oil, the smell of overheated electrics, courtesy of John's radio equipment - Adam got the scent of the perfumed soap Gerry used.

He gave Gerry a squeeze of his shoulder as he got to his feet. They'd done it now, they'd gone beyond the point of having doubts, now they were committed, they couldn't be half-hearted, they had to work together as a team to give themselves the best chance. He patted John on the shoulder, gave him a thumbs up and grasped the hand of Roland as he rose to go forward to his navigation station.

He looked for Leslie, had Howard gone? No, he was still sat with his back to the main spar, his face a pale blur in the blackness. He seemed not to have noticed that they were all going to their positions.

Should he leave him be? Gerry would, that was one of his failings, he'd go out of his way to avoid confrontation. Adam was different. Instead of heading to his lonely eyrie at the very rear of the aircraft, he leant down to the bomb aimer.

'It's time, Leslie,' he yelled.

The man didn't move. It was like he hadn't heard.

Puzzled, Adam reached out and shook his shoulder. Now there was a reaction; Howard jerked his head as if startled from sleep. He stared up at Adam.

'Positions, Leslie,' Adam yelled again. 'You need to be up front.'

Still he did not move, at least not at first. At last, though, he rose to his feet but still didn't move forward. What was going on?

'Leslie! Come on!' he said, leaning in close.

This time there was movement. Howard clambered over the spar and vanished into the darkness.

Adam shook his head. What was that all about? Well, he had his own job to do, he turned towards the tail. His foot got caught in something and he stumbled, banging his knee. Cursing, he groped back to find out what it was. His hand closed around something familiar; the strap of a parachute pack.

It had to be Leslie's.

'Bloody idiot,' he muttered to himself. He considered chasing after Howard but then thought of an alternative. He groped for the side of the fuselage and, within a few seconds found the microphone jack point. He plugged in and found that Roland was talking.

'- and turn right onto 087, Skip.'

'I want to fly a more direct route, make up time.'

There was a pause.

'That's not our orders, Dag.'

'Our orders were to take off fifty minutes ago. We need to get there sooner.'

'But-'

Adam couldn't wait. 'Skip, rear gunner here.'

'What is it?' The pilot's voice was filled with annoyance. 'What's wrong? You're not in the turret, are you? The trim's not changed.'

Adam was impressed. Even under stress, Dag had been able to feel exactly where his crew were.

'I'm going, Skip but Howard's left his parachute back here. He should be passing you. Someone tell him, would they?'

'For fuck's - Right. Burt, grab that idiot would you. Taylor, get to your turret.'

'Wilko, Skip. Out.'

Great. He'd only been trying to help and he'd been given a flea in his ear for his pains. So much for being a team.

He grasped his own parachute pack and headed back.

Gerry was already in his turret and was swinging around in it. Adam stepped past, staggering as the aircraft bumped through some turbulence just as he passed the Elson, bringing him closer to the sickly, chemical scent than he'd like. He knelt, feeling for the parachute clipping point on the fuselage side. Finding it and leaving his pack there, he undid the rear door to the turret, turned and fed himself, feet first, inside, into the seat. He closed the door. He was there, in his cold plastic and metal box, vulnerable and isolated.

He tried not to think about it.

He plugged in.

'Rear gunner,' he said. 'Coms check.'

LMF 45

26/1/44 10.35 pm

'Er, excuse me, radio operator here, er, crew, can the rest of you do a coms check?'

Gerry was about to reply but was interrupted.

'Hiley, for fuck's sake, get a grip. If you need something done just ask. Get the check done and clear the chatter, understand?'

'Yes, Skipper, sorry.'

'Pass on anything you hear from control or the bomber stream, that's all.'

'Yes sir.'

Gerry pulled a face in the darkness. Poor little John. He sounded like he needed a hug.

'Mid-upper gunner, coms check, please.'

Gerry pressed his mic button. 'Loud and clear, John, over.'

'Thank you, Gerry. Navigator, coms check.'

Gerry half listened whilst John went through the checks with the rest of the crew. All called in with one exception: Howard.

'Bomb aimer, coms check,' John repeated for the

fourth time.

'Howard, damn you, answer!' Dag's voice was harsh.

'I don't think he's plugged in.'

That was Saunders, the navigator.

'Well give him a kick up the arse. Useless fucker. You chose really well there, didn't you?'

'I don't have time. I'm taking a sight.'

'Kick him when you get back then.'

Gerry grimaced. This wasn't getting any better. Dag and the navigator were supposed to be friends, weren't they but the pilot had done nothing but snipe at him. This wasn't a happy ship at all. Still, they had to persevere, what other choice did they have? Keep going, do the normal things.

He pressed his mic button again. 'Permission to test the guns, Skip.'

'Yup, carry on. You too, Taylor.'

'Right, Skip.'

Gerry grasped the gun controls and used the foot pedals to swing the turret around. He felt the slipstream buffet and churn as it turned, these twin-gun Boulton-Paul turrets were like barn doors, most had been replaced by more cramped, streamlined ones but not C-Charlie. Still, old Charlie had survived up to now, so he must be doing something right.

Gerry patted the perspex. 'Keep lucky, Charlie,' he muttered and then pressed the triggers.

The thin lines of tracer arced out into the sky as the guns rattled and the turret filled with the sour acridness of cordite. The sensations gave Gerry a familiar lift that was almost sexual, he'd never told anyone about this, it wasn't something he could be proud about.

About twenty feet behind, Adam was also firing. His

turret had four guns and he was shooting upwards, the bullets streaking high then curving lazily down.

'That's enough. Don't advertise our position.'

'Sure, Skip,' said Gerry.

'Damn it! I've got a - no, wait. What's going on?'

'What is it, Adam?'

There was a pause.

'The ruddy turret jammed. It stuck,' he said at last. 'It's cleared now though. It was bloody spooky - it's not good.'

'Stop the chatter. Keep quiet and keep your eyes peeled.'

'But, if the turret's -'

'Enough, I said. Keep quiet. Do your job.'

There was another few seconds of silence.

'Yes, Skip.'

Adam was seething, Gerry could tell.

Was that it then? Adam wasn't to investigate further? Apparently not.

Gerry rotated his turret, quartering the night sky as C-Charlie climbed higher. Despite his electrically heated suit he was getting colder.

LMF 46

'C-Charlie climbed to its allocated altitude and followed the same route as the other bombers in the stream.'

26/1/44 10.38 pm

On the way back from the astrodome Roland briefly glanced at Dag and nodded to Burt in passing, but the engineer seemed intent on his instruments.

He was not convinced by the Australian. He didn't know him well but had heard rumours about Harrison being a heavy drinker. That wasn't unusual in a front-line squadron, everyone had different ways of getting through their tours, Roland included. The engineer's performance today was not reassuring though. He hoped he was paying more attention now.

Roland descended the steps into the nose. C-Charlie, like many of the older MK II Halifaxes, had been built with a front turret but this had been removed and fared over with aluminium, leaving the bottom perspex bomb aimer's position and no front gun, not even the single 'scarecrow' machine gun that others carried to discourage any attacker coming in from the front. Few ever did, which was why the turret had been deleted, that and the need to save weight and reduce drag to give the poor old Halifax the chance to climb higher and be a little safer, but it added to the feeling of vulnerability.

Roland felt it in his 'office' tucked away on the left-hand side under the floor on the pilot's side, but it was worse for the bomb aimer. He had to lie on his belly on the unarmoured metal skin of the aircraft during the run in to the target, peering through the bombsight which, itself, looked through the flat optical glass panel set in the lower part of the nose.

This was just one of the reasons Roland had switched to became a navigator in the first place. It was not, though, the major one. Although his training had gone well, he knew, deep down, that being the man to press the button that released the deadly load onto other human beings was not something he could countenance. It was a step too far.

He was glad that this was Howard's job.

Howard, though, was not doing his job. He was supposed to keep a watch out on the night sky that was rushing past his position but, instead, Roland could see that he was sat, head down almost between his knees, his back against the port side of the nose, parachute alongside him.

'Leslie!' Roland yelled. 'Leslie, are you all right?'

Howard raised his head. In the moonlight his features were clear. To Roland's surprise - and shock - he could see that the man's cheeks were wet. He was crying.

He bent over him, put his mouth to Howard's ear.

'What's wrong, old chap?' he said.

'I can't do it, I can't do it,' Leslie said. 'I'm not up to this, I'm just not.'

Roland took a deep breath. Howard had used the very words that he'd said to himself, so many times. How many? He couldn't count that high. He'd been able to drive them away each time, now he had to do the same to someone else.

'Come on, Leslie,' he said. 'Of course you can.'

'I can't, I tell you, I can't. We've got to turn back, we have to.'

This was going to take some time, time that Roland, in truth, didn't have. He had to plot their position, make drift calculations, update the course to the pilot. But he had to make time, he had no choice.

He made to sit down, moving Howard's parachute out of the way but the latter grabbed hold of it.

'No, no, I need that,' he yelled, snatching it back and cuddling it to his chest like a teddy bear.

Roland did not fight him over it. Wearily he slumped down alongside Howard, on the nose side, his legs arched over the bombsight.

'Come on, old man,' he said. 'Snap out of it. We all feel like you do.'

'You do? Everyone?'

'Oh yes, believe me, we do,' said Roland, as he settled down to do the best job of persuasion that he could manage.

LMF 47

S omething was wrong with the instruments.

They wouldn't keep still, they were wandering around his panel - which, he knew, was bloody stupid, it couldn't be right.

Burt screwed his eyes tight shut, took a deep breath and then opened them again. The dash had settled down, everything was where it should be. He sighed in relief and quickly scanned the dials, looking for any that were out of sync with the rest.

But they started shimmering again, swirling, drifting. Again he shut his eyes, rubbed them, red flashes exploding on his retinas, bursts of scarlet that faded and merged with the darkness.

Not all of them faded. Some stayed, not flashes but red dots, fireflies in the darkness, getting bigger. Eight of them, in pairs, in a straight line.

He had seen them before, but when?

'Height, Harrison?'

The fireflies went out, the instruments returned.

'Height, man! Wake up, what's our height?'

Dag's voice got through.

'Sorry, Skip. Crossing seven thousand.'

'About bloody time. Crew to oxygen. Report when you've done it.'

'Rear gunner, on oxygen, over.'

'Mid-upper, done it, Skip.'

'Radio operator, on oxygen, sir.'

'Same here, Skip,' said Burt. He waited for the other two.

There was silence.

'Howard! Roland!' Dag shouted. 'Where the bloody hell are you?'

'I don't think they're plugged in, Skip,' said Burt, peering into the nose.

'That's bloody obvious. I need my blasted navigator. Go and give them a nudge.'

'Right, Skip.'

Burt unplugged his oxygen line again. He decided there was no need to take his mobile bottle, they were below ten thousand and he'd only be a moment. He'd be fine.

He headed down the steps into the nose.

The fireflies, they were back. He'd seen them before, where?

They danced now, broke apart, bloomed, tumbled, dispersed.

Something dark loomed over him, he flinched, cowering away.

'You alright, Burt?'

He stared blankly at the shape.

'I'm guessing Dag will be going spare? Leslie felt a bit airsick but he's fine now.'

The shape resolved. Saunders, the navigator, settling back into his seat. Howard, the bomb aimer, moving into position.

'Oh right, mate, good stuff. The Skip wants everyone on oxygen.'

'No problem.'

Problem. Everyone had their problems. He had swirling instruments and fireflies. And Mags and the kids.

'Burt?'

Saunders was leaning over him.

'What?'

'Shouldn't you be getting back?'

'Oh yeah, sorry.'

Burt made his way back and plugged in. Instantly he heard Dag's voice.

'- the fuck have you been, Howard? No, fuck it, don't bother. Roland, where's my course?'

'Give me a minute, Dag.'

'Jesus Christ! Bloody well get on with it.'

Burt sighed. This wasn't a happy crew. Not like F-Freddie.

In front of him the instruments swirled and shifted.

LMF 48

26/1/44 10.50 pm

I t was cold in the cockpit, but Douglas was sweating.

It was not surprising, it felt like he was doing seven jobs, not just one. He was carrying the whole aircraft on his shoulders. Was it too much to ask that everyone else should pull their weight?

But hadn't that always been the case? His mother, a lush, always drunk, never there to look after him. His father forever flitting in and out, only staying over occasionally but his visits were something to dread, the stiff awkwardness over breakfast, the effect on his mother after he had gone.

The taunts at school, the names he first didn't understand but quickly came all-too familiar with. 'Daddy's little secret', 'Chambermaid's shame', 'The bastard'. It all got worse when his tormentors found they could get a reaction from him, that he was quick to resort to his fists and feet.

'You even fight like a little bastard,' one had whispered in his ear as he was dragged away after one scuffle. And then the boy had said, more loudly, 'Daddy will never invite you to his house, will he? His wife wouldn't like it.'

Douglas shook himself. Why did he have to keep dragging up the past? There was no need to, he was his own man, self-reliant, he didn't need anyone.

He didn't need anyone? What about Connie?

Well, there was a lesson for him. People, however

much you trusted them, would always let you down. He'd trusted Connie, he'd trusted Roland. Roland? Roly. What kind of name was that, anyway? A stuck-up name, typical of his type, his class, all just in it for themselves. How could he ever think that he could be a true friend?

And here he is, in person, the little Quaker. Leaning in close, wanting to talk off the intercom. Whispering his lies.

'About Howard,' he said. 'He had a bit-'

'I don't bloody care. What the fuck are *you* doing? Where's my bloody course?'

Roland looked surprised.

'I needed to -'

'You needed to do your damned job. Give me a fucking course. Cut a few corners. Quickest possible route in.'

'But -'

'Just do it, understand?'

'Yes, Skip.'

Roland, his face fixed, headed back to his station.

Right, good. Everyone was back doing their job. That was all he asked, he was doing his, was it too much to ask that everyone just did theirs?

'Skip? Mid-upper, over.'

Now what?

'What is it?'

'Skip, we're trailing vapour from the port outer.'

Shit.

'Vapour? What sort of vapour?'

'Could be smoke, Skip.'

'Well which is it? Smoke or vapour?'

'I don't know, Skip, I'm not an engineer, I'm just a gunner.'

Douglas took a deep breath. No, no, no, what the hell else was going to go wrong?

'Well get back to doing that. Burt, what are we looking at here?'

LMF 49

R oland, back in his seat having taken a sighting from the astrodome, completed his calculations and drew the course line in on the map. There'd been some drift, the winds were probably strong.

He should check.

He pressed the intercom switch.

'John, Roland here. Any reports of strong winds?'

'Yes, Roland. The stream's reporting north-westerlies, 40 to 50 knots at 15,000, over.'

'Keep the chatter down, you two.'

Dag; still furious. That was unfair, John was doing a great job. Well, sod him.

'Thanks, John,' he said.

'What's happening with the smoke, Skip?'

'I told you, keep the chatter on the com down. We'll let you know.'

That was Gerry, the gunner, and Dag's curt reply.

Smoke? What smoke? He must have missed something when he was in the astrodome. What was going on?

He didn't have long to wait for an answer.

'Right, listen up.' Dag again. 'We're trailing a bit of

smoke from the port outer but the gauges are fine. It'll probably be just the oil from the leak burning off. It won't affect us so we're pressing on. Skipper out.'

That was all right then. Yes, residual oil, that made sense.

He stopped amid his calculations. Did it make sense though? The oil had been mopped up, well mainly. Surely what was left would have burned off by now? Still, he wasn't an engineer and it was not his concern.

'Navigator to flight deck.'

Dag's call came as a surprise. He'd just been there. He pressed his talk button.

'What is it, Skip? I'm almost ready with your course.'

'I need you up here, now.'

Roland mentally shrugged, plugged into his mobile oxygen bottle, and ventured out again, blinking as his eyes adjusted to the darkness.

At the top of the steps he found the engineer bent over the instruments, a scrap of paper in hand, scribbling something down. Dag beckoned him over, then pulled his oxygen mask off as Roland got close enough to hear.

'Don't say anything on the intercom,' Dag yelled over the clamour in the cockpit. 'The leak from the port outer is bad. Oil pressure is dropping.'

He pulled his mask back on.

Roland just stared at him for a few moments. That was not what Dag had said to the rest of the crew. He'd lied.

He removed his own mask.

'Shouldn't we scrub?'

Dag shook his head before removing his mask again. 'No, we're not scrubbing, not after coming this far.'

'So why -'

'We need to shorten the trip,' Dag interrupted, and, for Roland, it all fell into place. 'We need to get as close as we can on all four. After we've bombed we'll be less vulnerable on three. We can shut it down then.'

Dag put his mask back on. He was breathing deeply and, now Roland's night vision had come fully back and he could see the look in Dag's eyes; They were pleading, you owe me this, they said, don't let me down.

'You want a direct course?' He said.

Dag nodded.

Roland found himself doing the same.

Dag immediately turned back to flying. That was it, the decision had been made.

As Roland made his way back he glanced at the haggard engineer, then back into the depths of the aircraft where John, Gerry and Adam were at their stations. He owed them a duty as much as he did Dag, he owed it them to keep them safe. What was he doing now then?

He was putting them at risk, that was clear. If he did what Dag asked, he would be going against the briefing, moving off the route that should keep them going in the same direction as all the other machines. Although the sky was big this would be like driving down the wrong side of the road in total darkness with the lights off. And all to cover a greater risk, an engine whose life fluids were leaking away, whose condition he was conspiring with Dag and Harrison to keep the truth from the rest of the crew.

This wasn't fair, it wasn't right, they should have a say.

But he did owe Dag. He'd betrayed him. He should betray him again, tell the crew. Tell John, Gerry, Adam and Leslie. Let them decide.

He plugged into the intercom, looked at his chart,

then switched his mic on.

'Skipper, steer 175,' he said.

LMF 50

'The navigation log shows that the crew then made an unscheduled and unsanctioned course change that took C-Charlie on a more direct route over occupied Holland.'

26/1/44 11.20 pm

'That's the Dutch coast ahead, Skipper.'

'Crew: Enemy coast ahead. Keep your eyes peeled.'

Howard's stomach lurched. He could not forget how little separated him from that hostile world, the perspex, less than a quarter inch of it, thin gauge aluminium all around him. He might as well be naked.

It was so unfair, it sent a message to him and all the others in bomber command who did his job, a very clear message: 'You're not worth the effort to protect, you're expendable, old chap'.

Not like the fighter boys, oh dear no. He'd once sat in a Spitfire and the jealousy had worsened. Behind the seat was thick armour plate protecting the pilot's back and head. In front of him was the massive V12 Merlin engine and armoured glass to look through. Pilots were cosseted, protected, cherished.

Valued.

He wasn't. He was in the most vulnerable position in the most vulnerable of targets.

It wasn't meant to be this way.

He was meant to be a pilot, a fighter pilot. That was what his father had in mind for him.

'One of the boys in blue, the few, excellent, my boy, excellent.'

That's what his father had said. He'd even given his son a rare pat of praise on the shoulder. It was a moment that Howard had treasured for months.

He'd got used to failing, that was the bitter truth. He was useless at sports, useless at school. He knew he wasn't brave, however much he wanted to be. He couldn't measure up to his father's expectations but, then, the bar was so high who could possibly meet them? Everyone told him how much they admired his father and the fact that he'd won the VC; Howard found himself wishing that the old man had been killed.

He had conditioned himself to always falling short, to criticism, to sighs and looks of disappointment.

Those looks reappeared when he'd been allocated to bomber pilot training rather than fighters. 'You'll be nothing but a glorified bus driver,' his father had said and refused to be placated by his son's argument that it was only bomber command that was truly taking the war to the Nazis and that bomber pilots were selected for their leadership qualities.

Father and son had barely talked that leave, even though Howard was due to sail the next morning.

Howard thought of the weeks in Canada when he'd been unable to bring himself to write home to break the news that, after twenty hours of flight training, he'd not reached the required standard, and that he was not going to be a pilot at all.

He was offered the alternatives of training as a navigator or bomb aimer. He'd chosen the latter for no good reason, he'd been in a daze of shame. He'd let his father down again. When he finally did write it had been six weeks before he'd received a short reply that said little in words but much in what was omitted.

He had failed again. And now he was failing at this. Talking to Saunders had helped but now, on his own again he was facing his demons and the demons were winning. He was rushing towards the flak, the shrapnel, the bullets, the shells, protected only by his thin plastic and metal cocoon.

The dark line that was the coast, fringed by the white of breaking waves, passed beneath him. Immediately, streaks of white, orange and yellow started to arc up towards him.

He closed his eyes and tried not to be sick.

LMF 51

'Light flak was encountered as the aircraft crossed the enemy coast.'

26/1/44 11.24 pm

T he aircraft rocked, John's pencil slipped on the paper as he tried to transcribe the morse coming through his headset.

What was it? Turbulence?

Then he heard the thump-crump and he realised that he was under fire. For the first time in his life someone was actively trying to kill him.

His eyes went to the patch on the aircraft's skin, only eighteen inches away. Some other man had sat where he did, doing the job he was doing now, when a white-hot piece of metal had torn through there and through him. Would he have known anything about it? Would it have hurt? Did he know that this could have happened whilst he sat there? No, that was stupid, of course he would have known. So how had he stayed there knowing that?

And now, could John?

No, he could not think like that. He couldn't think about it at all if he was to do his job.

Which he wasn't doing. Whilst he was brooding he'd missed the last few seconds of morse.

He forced himself to listen again. Concentrating on transcribing helped him stop shaking.

The pathfinders were over the target now. They were having difficulty marking, the winds were strong and clouds at lower levels kept obscuring the target. The flak -

A massive bang drowned out the bleeps, a sound like gravel flung against a metal barrel. C-Charlie lifted, then dropped. John was suddenly weightless, his pencil, ruler and pad floated in the air, hung there for what seemed like seconds but were probably mere moments, then were flung back to the table. John himself dropped, missing his seat and landing painfully on the floor.

He scrambled to get in his chair again.

'Christ.'

'What was that?'

'Stop the chatter, everyone. Any damage? Report in.'

'Rear gunner. All alright here, skipper.'

'Mid-upper. That was close. My canopy's got a crack in it but seems okay. I'm okay too.'

'Navigator. I'm alright.'

John knew he should reply but he was transfixed by something. There was something dark dripping onto his pad. Puzzled, he moved his light. The drips were red. It was blood, sticky and stiff in the cold.

Where had it come from? It had to be his blood but from where, he'd not felt anything. He started to check himself all over.

'Radio operator. Bomb aimer. Report in!'

'Bomb aimer. Yes, I'm fine.'

There was another thump. C-Charlie bumped and lurched.

'John? Are you all right?'

Saunders. He was asking about him. The fog lifted.

John flicked his intercom switch. 'Sorry, I was taking morse. I think I'm fine.'

'Well you either are or you're not, which is it? Oh forget it, navigator, can you find a way through?'

The skipper. Cross as usual.

'We'll be over the islands in a few minutes and clear of the coast defences. I'll give you a new course then.'

'You do that. Howard, keep an eye out for flak ships whilst we're over the inland sea.'

Silence.

'Bomb aimer! Wake up you useless sod.'

'Sorry. Will do.'

John had not found the source of the blood. Was it possible to be hit badly, mortally, and yet not feel it? Probably not, but he still felt faint.

Stop that, he told himself. The others were relying on him. He couldn't let them down.

He tried to concentrate on his morse transcription.

His pad kept spotting with blood.

LMF 52

26/1/44 11.35 pm

'Alter course to 155, Skipper.'

'155.'

Gerry rotated his turret, quartering the sky as C-Charlie's port wing dipped to complete the turn.

He had hours of this to go but already his eyes were burning, sore and tired. At least his heartbeat had returned to normal.

The flak had been a shock, it had been one of the closest bursts he could remember, the shell exploding above and to port whilst he had the turret pointing to starboard. The reddish-yellow flash and the double crack of the report and the shrapnel impacting his canopy had been virtually simultaneous.

It had rattled him, there was no doubt about that, in fact rattled was an understatement. He'd thought it was the end, he'd screamed, come close to soiling himself. He hoped that he'd not pressed the mic button, that nobody had heard his panic.

He was fine now though, back to normal, doing his job, protecting the crew.

His crew.

This wasn't his crew though was it? His team, his friends. His love.

Once his love, now gone.

Had it been like that for John, the other John, a flak burst like that one but worse, tearing into them, destroying them? If it was then there was nothing that he or Adam could have done. You can't fight off flak, it comes at you out of the night, a swinging hammer blow. If it was that he couldn't have let them down, could he? It would make no difference whether he was there or not.

He was fooling himself, wasn't he though? Trying to make it right.

It wasn't alright. It never could be. He couldn't know how they died, no one could, there were no witnesses. For as long as he lived his guilt would haunt him.

So what could he do? Nothing, just carry on as best as he could. That and keep the last survivor of *his* crew as safe as he could.

He rotated his turret to the rear so he could see Adam's. It was moving from side to side. He was still fine, that was good. Gerry had to try and keep him like that.

And to do that he had to stay alert. He rotated the turret to the left, checking the upper quarter of the sky. The coastal flak was behind them but now they were in the night fighter belt, they had to be even more vigilant.

Not that the peashooters they carried were much use. The Brownings were all right but they lacked punch. He'd followed current thinking and loaded a higher percentage of armour piercing bullets than the RAF armourers recommended, in fact he'd constant fights with the gunnery officers over it. 'You'll wear out the barrels too quickly, we'll have to keep replacing them,' one had grumbled. It had been Adam that had delivered the rejoinder: 'If we're scattered in bits over Germany then you'll have more than the barrels to replace, won't you?'

Gerry still smiled at the thought. Adam could still

come to his rescue. That felt good.

But that didn't change the fact that the fighters still out-gunned them. They could stand beyond the range of the Brownings and still shoot them down. Nor that Adam's displays of brotherhood had been rare since...well, since his brothers had died.

Grimly, Gerry rotated the turret. The port outer was still smoking. Surely it should have stopped by now? He was about to get on the intercom, to tell the skipper, when something stopped him. Something, he couldn't put it more than that, had attracted his attention.

Ahead of them. What was it? Had he seen a movement, was it a cloud changing shape? Or something else?

He switched his mic on.

'Skipper...'

That was as far as he got before a huge black shape flashed close over the top of his turret.

C-Charlie lurched violently down and to the right.

Gerry's head hit the side of his canopy with a flash of red and pain.

LMF 53

Adam's hands were torn from his gun controls. He was like a rag doll, unable to control his limbs, let alone free himself from his turret and get to his parachute. It was the sum of all his fears; battered, helpless, pinned by centrifugal forces, in a situation where it was impossible to escape but where he was aware of his fate.

He'd had this nightmare before. But now it was real.

All he could do was push his terror, the certainty of his fate, away so he could picture Sarah, find peace in her image and solace for his last moments.

But even this slight comfort would not come. In its stead was a melange of condemnation, rage, loss, guilt and shame - at his situation, his powerlessness and, above all, at his complicity in his own demise.

LMF 54

Howard was suddenly pressed against the frame of the nose and the perspex hemisphere, discovering every protuberance and projection into the interior space, tattooing his body with bruises, leaving painful mementos.

Not that he would live long enough to see them.

This was it, this was how it ended, his life would close full of pain, pinned, helpless, the roar of the engines drowned out by that of the blood in his head and the scream of the air forced over C-Charlie as it plunged and twisted downwards.

The aircraft would come apart, it had to, it couldn't stand this. Would it tear him up with it when it did? Perhaps he'd be flung clear?

No. He was never that lucky.

LMF 55

26/1/44 11.38 pm

John's world was a swirling snowstorm of paper and pencils with red blobs floating where his eye had impacted with the dials of his radio.

He was oddly detached amidst the chaos, like he was observing himself from outside. He tried to work out how he had got in this position. Ah, yes, that must be it, he'd caught his knee under his table and it had pinwheeled him around, planting his face against his own wireless. And what he kept bouncing off wasn't the floor, it was the roof of the cabin.

He was glad he was still rational. That was good. He could breathe too, and hear. Yells, cries, the banging of loose equipment, the scream of the air rushing past outside a scant inch or so above his head, the creaks and cracks from the structure of the aircraft.

There was a strange smell too. Above the petrol, oil, paint and metal was something different, something odd. A sweet, chemical smell. What was it?

Would he ever know? He didn't want to die not knowing, but then there were so many things that he did not know and had not done.

It was all so unfair.

LMF 56

26/1/44 11.38 pm

Every trip Roland had done he had wondered what it would feel like to get shot down. Well, now he knew.

Flak or cannon fire? He hadn't heard firing, so it had to be flak. Yet he hadn't heard that either, he hadn't expected that.

But then he also hadn't expected to go out tangled in the curtain that screened his navigation position, nor with the smell of the Elson strong in his nostrils.

It was all too distracting. He wanted Connie to be the last thing he remembered.

LMF 57

26/1/44 11.39 pm

'Come on, you bitch, come on!'

'Airspeed, watch the airspeed.'

'I'm watching it, there's fuck all I can do - wait, she's coming back. Throttle back the...starboard...engines.'

Douglas was panting with the exertion. The Halifax was a heavy beast to fly at the best of times but now he was straining every sinew to force the control yoke over, his muscles the only things that, via the control cables, were forcing the ailerons to move against the tortured, rushing air-flow. Similarly, his left foot was jammed hard down on the rudder pedal, against the direction of the spin.

It had been disorientating, terrifyingly confusing in the darkness, a swirling, twisting, tearing assault on the senses. He had been shocked into inaction during the first few moments as C-Charlie was torn from his grasp then lifted upward, over and down. Down and spinning round and around.

But now she was -

'Full throttle, port engines!'

'But -'

'Do it!'

The horizon, indistinct as it was, was settling, the rotation was slowing. It was accompanied by heavy thumps from behind him, distinct even over the roar of the airflow rushing over the airframe and cockpit. He had other things to worry about, they were not out of the woods yet; the altimeter was rapidly unwinding as the airspeed indicator moved towards its stops.

'Oh Christ, oh Jesus Christ, no!'

'Quiet, Burt. Throttle back, do it!'

The engineer did nothing. Douglas reached across and pulled the throttles on the left side of the quadrant back to idle, then braced himself and hauled back on the stick. It was like pulling against concrete.

'Help me, Burt, for fuck's sake, help me.'

The engineer appeared frozen, catatonic, staring out into the rushing darkness. Douglas cursed him and continued to heave back on the near rigid controls.

Near but not complete. He felt the yoke move slightly. Was it enough? The airspeed indicator was winding back, only a little bit, but they were definitely slowing as the air grew thicker, but then the strain on the structure was growing. He really needed -

A second pair of hands joined him on the yoke, helping him to heave back. Douglas glanced across, it was Roland, wide-eyed, clearly shaken, but there alongside him.

And, together, they were winning, the nose was lifting, yes, it was coming up. The airframe creaked, groaned, it sounded horrible, audible even over the rushing air but then this too started to fade. The altimeter stabilized, stopped, then started to rise again.

'Right,' he said. 'That's it. We should be okay now. Thanks.'

Roland let go of the controls and just nodded.

'Burt!' he yelled at the engineer. 'Burt, come on, man!'

Roland reached out and shook the Australian's shoulder. This seemed to rouse him, though he looked confused.

'Sorry, Skip,' he said.

'Throttle's to cruise - no, hell, we're below three thousand, we need to climb. Full throttle.'

Light flak was already starting.

Harrison reached towards the controls but hesitated.

'What about the port outer?' he said.

'We can't spare it. If we don't get higher we're dead anyway.'

'Yes, Skip.'

'Keep an eye on it though.' He looked at Roland. 'You all right?'

'Yes. A bit knocked about but I'm fine.'

'Good, I need a course.'

Roland stared at him. 'Home?' he said.

Douglas shook his head. 'No, the target. We're going on.'

LMF 58

'As a result, C-Charlie had to descend to avoid a collision with another, unknown aircraft... No damage occurred in this incident and the crew pressed on.'

26/1/44 11.39 pm

'**W**hat the hell was that? Are we all right?'

Who was that? Howard struggled to place the voice. What a stupid thing to say, how could they be all right after that?

His head was spinning as if the aircraft was still rotating. He was disoriented, confused and also soaked and stank. Why? Then he realised; he'd been sick, though he couldn't remember when. Disgusted, he tried to wipe the worst of it off his flight suit. Had it come to this, the son of a war hero soaked in his own vomit.

'Stop the chatter. Report in. Anyone injured? Any damage?'

'I feel like I've done ten rounds with Joe Louis.'

Battered, bruised, shamed. Howard felt just the same.

'Report properly. Are you injured?'

There was a pause.

'Rear gunner. I'm alright.'

'Mid-upper?'

'I'm alright...I think. Banged my head and my knees hurt, over.'

'Navigator here. I'm with John. He's hurt. I think he's broken his wrist.'

'Shit. That's all we need.'

That was the pilot. Howard's senses were coming back.

'Wait. He's wanting me to plug him back in. He wants a word.'

There was the sound of scratching through Howard's headset.

'Hello, Skipper. Radio Operator here. It's alright, I can manage. Sorry, I just fell badly.'

'Good man. Bomb aimer. How are you doing?'

There was no reply. The bomb aimer wasn't replying. Wait, HE was the bomb aimer. Where was his mask, with the microphone? It had come off. He found it hanging to one side.

'Hello Skipper, I'm here. I'm -'

'Right, good,' Dag interrupted. 'Everyone back to their stations. Navigator, leave John. I need that course for the target.'

There was a moment of silence. Howard couldn't believe what he'd just heard. It was soon obvious he was not alone.

'What? After that? You've got to be kidding, haven't you?'

'Taylor, that's enough. Of course we're going on. Why shouldn't we?'

'Because we just nearly dug our own graves in Germany, that's why. What was that anyway?'

'Another plane, Adam, a Lancaster, I think. Flying the other way. It nearly took my turret off.'

'What? What was it doing on a reciprocal course to the bomber stream - wait, what course were we on? Was it the briefed one?'

'Taylor, shut up. I've told you already. Keep quiet and do your job.'

'Fuck you, Dag, I am doing my job. Are you doing yours?'

'Enough!'

'No it's not enough, I want an answer. Saunders, were we on course - the *approved* course?'

'Well, er…'

'Yes or no?'

There was another long pause. Howard found he was holding his breath. Surely Saunders wouldn't have -

'No. We were taking a short cut. But, still, there shouldn't haven't been anything on that bearing tonight.'

The aircraft's communication system fell silent again.

'Why? Why would you do something like that? This fucking job is dangerous enough as it is.'

Taylor again.

'It was something that -'

'I ordered him to do it,' said Dag.

'I might have known. Well, I value my life even if you don't. Now turn this machine around.'

Yes, yes, yes, thought Howard, please do that.

'No,' said Dag. 'I'm in command. We're not damaged, we go on.'

No, thought Howard. No, no, no.

LMF 59

'Following the loss of altitude, C-Charlie attempted to climb back to its assigned bombing height.'

26/1/44 11.39 pm

G erry was shaking, barely able to keep his hands on his gun controls.

Every cloud, every tiny change in the light and, in his mind, he could see the black shape rushing out of the sky towards him.

Perhaps it had touched some ancient primeval fears of the night, of witches, bats, deadly wraiths, inhabitants of the nightmare lands between the real world and the imagined. Yet this fear was very real, modern, physical. It was several tons of aluminium, steel and perspex carrying seven bodies and travelling at a combined speed of, what? Four hundred miles an hour? Something like that.

If the other aircraft had been twenty feet lower...

Would he have felt anything? What happened to you if your life was snuffed out in an instant? He was full of memories, of everything he'd ever known, from the earliest he could date, of his grandfather who'd died when he was two, to his first day at school, his first kiss, falling in love for the first time and the intensity of pain when it was over, some vivid, some vague, how could they all suddenly cease to exist?

Yet that was what death must be like, wasn't it? The end of everything for the individual. A full stop. Over and out.

But there were alternative thoughts weren't there? On

death and the afterlife? How many of his childhood Sundays were spent in church? Too many, but how much could he remember?

'Skipper, radio operator here, over.'

Gerry's reflections were interrupted by John's voice. C-Charlie's crew had fallen silent since the furious exchange between Adam and the Skipper. He guessed that, like himself, everyone had been lost in their own thoughts.

'Yes, John, what is it?'

'Signal from HQ, relayed from the Master Bomber. Flak is very heavy and accurate over the target, particularly below Angels One Four. Recommend bomb at higher level if possible. That's it, Skipper. Over.'

There were a few seconds of silence. The rest of the crew would probably be thinking what he was; height was the one thing they did not have. What height could they get to in the run into the target? Sure, they were climbing again now, but they were so low and climbing slowed them, keeping them in the nightfighter belt for longer.

The trip had started badly and was getting worse.

'Thanks, John. Skipper out.'

That was it. No change. They were going on.

John was such a lovely lad. Saunders had strapped his wrist up and he'd insisted on carrying on. He must be in agony. Gerry wished he could give him a hug.

But no, he couldn't do that, he couldn't go there again. He needed to bury his feelings.

Could he though? He certainly couldn't bury his fears, couldn't forget the deadly shadows in the night.

Was there any solace to be found in the church? What could he remember? Jesus was the way, the truth and the light, and, and this was the important bit, whoever believed in him would have eternal life, even if they died.

Even if they died. He didn't want to die but, still, if he did, that appealed. Life afterwards, a continuation.

Was it too late to start believing?

How did you start?

The Lord's prayer, that was a good a place as ever.

'Our Father, who art in heaven,' he muttered to himself, as he continued to quarter the sky for evil.

LMF 60

T here was snow on the ground. Adam only slowly registered the fact but, once he had, the implications hit him immediately. Their largely black aircraft would be clearly silhouetted against the pale ground when viewed from above. They were much lower than they should be, of course and, because they were climbing, they were moving more slowly than they would have been if they had been at their cruising altitude.

That made them very, very vulnerable. They were running a huge risk.

And why? Because they were all in the hands of an unbalanced pilot whose judgement was questionable. Adam had heard the gossip back in Cambridgeshire, normally he didn't listen, but it mattered who you flew with. It was why crews came together early to become a team, to understand each other, work together to improve, build trust and confidence.

So how many of this crew did he trust? How many did he have confidence in? Truthfully? None of them, not even Gerry. He was too eager to please people, to be accepted. As for the pilot -

A searchlight sprang up into the night sky from a point on the ground about 3 miles to the left of them, followed quickly by a second. The lights were searching for them. A line of tracer rose towards them , the gunners were firing blindly at the engine noise, Adam was sure, hoping for a lucky hit.

The rudders either side of his turret shifted as Dag edged C-Charlie to starboard, away from the immediate danger.

That was good, that was right, but it was just pilot's instinct. Any of them could do that. Dag was still pig-headed, cavalier with the lives of those who flew with him.

'Stop it,' he muttered to himself. He was angry, yes, and he had every right to be. He had something to live for, his wife and unborn child but he couldn't let that rage distract him. He was the eyes in a quarter that no one else in the aircraft could see, down and to the rear. He had to be professional, keep them all alive even if the rest weren't performing.

The searchlights and gun fell behind, the lights still impotently searching. The snow was thick, it looked bleak and exposed down there. It was cold enough up here but at least he had his heated suit, the enemy crews would be chilled to the bone, near frozen hands working the controls, the bitter wind going right through them.

Poor devils.

But why was he sympathising with them? They were trying to kill him and, despite his suit, he was cold and isolated, all rear gunners were the last line of defence in the most vulnerable part of the aircraft. This was the least survivable post in bomber command, it was hard to escape, and you just had to sit as the bullets and shells hurtled towards you from out of the darkness with nothing but a thin layer of perspex between you and satan.

So sod them, let them freeze. They were safe on the ground, trying to stop him getting home to Sarah and their firstborn.

Them and that crazy pilot, his crony the navigator, that bloody useless drunk of an engineer and the rest of them.

Stop it! Concentrate.

He mustn't let his anger distract him.

Light glowed in the clouds just above. Adam swung the turret around, elevating the guns, aiming at that point of the sky. What was it?

The truth was he knew. He had seen it before and, two or three seconds later his fears were confirmed. A large aircraft broke through the clouds about a mile away, burning, breaking up, falling.

And, illuminated in the flames was a second machine, smaller, stag like with antlers on its nose.

A creature of the night, an angel of death.

A nightfighter.

LMF 61

'Heavy going down to a fighter. Eight o'clock high, about a mile behind us.'

John recognised the rear gunner's voice.

'Oh God, it's alight from end to end.'

That was Gerry.

'Nevermind about them, where's the fighter? Can you see it?'

The skipper.

'Yes, it's lit up by the Lanc. I don't think it's seen us yet.'

'Well, keep an eye on it.'

'Wilco.'

John had been about to report. He had picked up wireless chatter: high winds and cloud over the target. He hesitated, not wanting to interrupt. The gunners might be about to give an urgent message, a warning to the pilot that could be the difference between life and death.

So, he'd wait, just note down the details and, if and when they were in the clear, he would report then.

He was pleased that he'd decided, it felt mature, grown up. He put down his headset and picked up the one for his radio, wincing as the bones in his wrist grated together.

Roland had done a fair job of strapping him up, his hand was stiff, but he was still able to hold a pencil and, with difficulty, write, albeit less neatly than normal.

He hoped they'd understand back at the base.

But, as soon as he had cut himself off from the rest of the crew he no longer felt grown up. He was alone in the darkness and the old fears came back.

He was never sure whether his fears were based on a genuine memory, an event from his early childhood or had just developed out of a particularly vivid dream, but the recurring image was of talons and a savagely hooked beak hurtling out of the gloom at him, ready to tear his flesh and pluck out his eyes. He remembered crying in terror, his parents comforting him, his mother reassuring him that there was no such thing as monsters but, when his light was switched off again, the fear returned.

That was just how he felt now. Turning off the internal radio was like turning off the light. He was alone in the darkness again.

But he was a man now, he shouldn't be afraid. He was eighteen, nearly nineteen, he should have outgrown it.

Yet he knew he hadn't. Anyway, these monsters of the dark were real. They were dark, like bats, and really did hide in the shadows ready to pounce. They were creatures of nightmare blindly feeling for their prey, keen to feed, to tear into their victim not with tooth and claw but explosive shells.

That was what had happened to the other aircraft. What would it have been like? Taylor had said it was a Lancaster - no surprise, they were more of them than Halifaxes - they were more cramped inside, harder to get out of. It had been burning from end-to-end, that was what Gerry had said. John had not been able to move when they'd spun out of control, it would have been worse for the Lanc crew, trapped inside an inferno.

It was horrific, almost too terrible to imagine but he

had and now he could not get the thoughts out of his head.

He had to. He had to concentrate and do his job.

He desperate to put the others back on, didn't want to be alone in the dark. There were monsters out there.

LMF 62

'Can you still see it, Adam?'

'Just about. It's a Junkers 88. It keeps disappearing into the cloud but then I pick it up again against the snow.'

'How has he not seen us?'

Burt had no bloody clue either. Why had he let himself be bullied into this? This was the worst trip he'd ever been on, a disaster in the making.

How much of the disaster was down to him though? He'd been a fair dinkum idiot not to have seen the oil leak, how the flaming hell had he not? Well, he hadn't so he just had to get on with it and do his job, didn't he?

But what was the point? This was hopeless, totally hopeless. They were too low, too slow, they should turn back, run, get out of there, head for home.

Home. Oh Mags, he was never going to see -

The kids, what would his kids do? They'd be orphaned, lose both of them, on the self-same night most like.

But, then, what were they missing? He was worse than his old man and that was saying something. Strewth, what a mess.

Stop it. Concentrate on the job, on that bloody engine.

What was it doing? He couldn't focus, his eyes were shot. He needed to get closer. Fuck, the oil pressure was right down, it would be overheating. How long was it going to last on this power? He should throttle it back, give it a break to make it last longer.

But then they'd be even lower and slower and -

'It's dark under the clouds and he's lower than us for now. He's getting closer though.'

'Don't fire at it. Don't do anything to give our position away.'

'For heaven's sake, Dag, we know that.'

'I'm not Dag to you. I'm the skipper and don't you bloody forget it.'

'How could we?'

'Yes, skipper.'

Joe in the rear turret was getting narked. No, not Joe. Joe was...gone. That was...what was his name? Who was their rear gunner? Had he ever known it? If he had it had gone from his head.

Like a lot of things. Other than Mags and the kids. It was all a jumble.

What was he about to do?

He had to keep his head, that's what. They'd have no chance if he didn't. He needed to keep the engines running, all the engines running for as long as possible. So what was next? The tanks! He'd have to do the fuel transfer soon, wouldn't he? When though? He was confused. It must have been the spin.

But he was confused before that, wasn't he?

He could really do with a drink. His flask was tucked into his tunic, he could feel it. His old captain didn't mind him taking the odd nip, but this one? He was a nasty, angry little bastard, a martinet. He'd say something.

Only if he knew. How would he know? He'd have a snorter whilst doing the tanks. Oh yes, he could taste it already, navy rum he had, the decent stuff.

The tanks. What were the levels? He bent forward to peer at the gauges.

'I've lost him. Can you still see him, Gerry?'

'No, Adam, I lost him a while back.'

'Shit, where's the bastard gone?'

'Pipe down, you two. Report in if you see something.'

'Yes, skip.'

They'd lost it, the useless bastards had lost it. It had seen them, he knew it, it would be stalking them, closing in for the kill. The kids would be orphans, destitute.

He needed that drink, he needed it now. He stepped away, pretending to write the consumption figures in his notebook but his hands were shaking too much to write. He'd been relying on experience and guesswork to get this far. He could barely hold the flask, but he managed to get the stopper off and find his mouth.

The rum burned but it was immediately better. Much better.

He took another swig.

LMF 63

'Some nightfighter activity was noted over the Dutch/German border.'

27/1/44 12.20 am

Howard was a prisoner, in fact it was worse than that; he was a condemned man waiting for the executioner. The act of execution was pure violence, but the anticipation was the real punishment. Death would be relief.

He shivered. Even a dank, dark condemned cell would be better than where he was right now. A cell would be solid and quiet, the condemned man would get some peace. Howard had no peace, he lay within a miserable cacophony jolted by a symphony of vibrations.

Above all, a condemned cell would not show the prisoner his future, a preview of hell. Fires on the ground, fire in the air, flashes, burning points of light falling to earth. Were they flares or falling planes? That glow, to the right of the nose, was the target. What was that, fifty or sixty miles away?

What a choice he had. Die here at the hands of the fighter or over there in the flak. It was madness, a wall of searchlights, battery after battery of guns throwing up luminous volleys of deadly metal. By the time they got to the city the guns would no longer have a choice of targets, it would almost certainly be just them. The gunners would be vengeful too, wanting to pay back the RAF for the damage, death and injury they had caused.

'Skipper, change course to one seven five.'

'Roger. One seven five.'

Howard felt the increase in weight as C-Charlie banked around to the right, placing the red hell that was their target right in the centre of the perspex hemisphere before him. This was it, they were going in, their final walk to execution.

He reached for his parachute, checked that the route to the hatch was clear. Could he get to it in time to bail out? Not if they were spinning, he'd already had a preview of that, he'd been pinned, unable to move.

The bile rose into his mouth.

He was dead, dead.

He turned to stare at the mouth of hell again. It was getting closer.

Howard thought of something, and, once he had, the thought would not go away.

What was the point of a bomber? That was simple; it was to drop bombs. If it had no bombs there was no point going on.

He felt for the bomb controls, the bay doors, the toggle to drop them. It was in his power to end this nightmare.

Unbidden, an image of his father's face came to him, that familiar expression; disappointment.

How was he supposed to measure up to his old man? He wasn't courageous. Or was he? To do this would require courage, a different form to his father's but courage, nonetheless.

Did he have it? Could he do it?

LMF 64

27/1/44 12.28 am

Well, that was it. They'd made the last course change, things were now out of his hands until they dropped their bombs.

If they got that far of course. He didn't know their height, but they had to be too low, they'd lost so much in the near-collision.

Was that his fault? Roland tried to be realistic, he had taken a risk with the course, but they'd been unlucky. He'd aimed for a narrow gap in Hitler's Atlantic wall where it was understood that the flak was a little lighter. He'd known about it because it had come up in briefings, so others would have known too. It was North of tonight's return route so there shouldn't have been anything on a reciprocal course but, of course, they shouldn't have been there either. It was just bad luck.

Roland sighed. There was one inescapable fact that; bad luck or not, they were there because he'd done what Dag had wanted: he was culpable. He'd conspired with him against the rest of the crew, put their lives at risk. And what about the other aircraft? They'd have been disturbed by slip-stream from C-Charlie as much as they had been, what if they'd crashed? It was possible they had. He had chosen the course, him. Had he just killed seven men?

More deaths to add to his conscience, because, despite his beliefs -

187

'Skipper, rear gunner.'

Roland's musings were interrupted.

'Yes, Taylor?'

'I thought I saw something after you made that last turn, slightly to port and behind us. I think we might have lost it but be ready to corkscrew to starboard.'

'Thanks, will do.'

So the fighter was still stalking them. If so, his course change had helped them this time.

What had he been thinking about? Oh, yes, of course, death, the ones on his conscience. Possibly the crew of the Lancaster, certainly all those he'd killed on previous raids and those to come, the ones that would die due to the load that was held in the belly of C-Charlie.

But he had always known this. Yes, he was a Quaker, he believed in peace but also that this was a justified war against a greater evil. Still, he'd had to switch from his original training as a bomb aimer to navigation in order to be able to live with himself, to kid himself that it was not him doing the killing. He'd enjoyed the discipline of bomb aiming, the maths, the calculations, the careful, studious qualities required, it suited his character, but, even in training, when he came to press the tit and drop the bombs, then the reality of what he would have to do hit home. He had known he could not do it and had immediately requested the switch.

Roland frowned, something had occurred to him, something he would not have thought about if he'd not been thinking about bomb aiming. Howard hadn't fused the bombs, had he? If he had, Roland hadn't seen him do it, he'd have had to go back to do it ,and passed him. He must have forgotten.

He reached for the intercom switch then stopped. Dag would blow his top if he heard, was wound up enough as it was, anyway. Roland didn't want to risk interrupting the gunners. He'd just leave his position and go and remind Howard.

As he left his seat, he prayed that C-Charlie would not start corkscrewing just at that moment.

LMF 65

27/1/44 12.29 am

'Come on, come on, come on, come on.'

Douglas realised he was muttering to himself but didn't stop, it was helping to divert some of the nervous energy coursing through him. It was like every nerve ending was on fire, like he was crackling with electricity. He needed to do something physical to consume some of it, to run, wave his arms around, even to dance but, of course, he couldn't, he had to stay at the controls unable to escape from the tension building within him.

It was almost unbearable.

Almost, but the target was there, he could see it now, a red scar filling the windscreen, on the ground and repeated and reflected by the clouds above. It was more than a target, it was the end of this phase of his life. Get there and he'd be done, he could get away, he didn't care where as long as it wasn't here.

Away from Connie, that was over too. It was not the ending he had expected, but what did he expect? He'd trusted her, trusted Roland too, when, throughout his life he'd learned no one could be relied on. Not a mother to stay sober, not a father to stay and see him as more than an irritation and a drain on his finances.

A red light flashed on his dashboard. Red for danger. The boozer, the Monica tail warning radar. Please, not now, he thought.

Something was searching for them, sending out electronic feelers into the night. It had found them, it was toying with them.

He felt for his intercom switch.

'Crew, the boozer's flashing. Prepare for corkscrew.'

There was no reply, they knew better. Everyone would be on edge, ready for action, for the call.

The light still flashed.

'Leave me alone, you bastard,' he muttered. 'I'm nearly there.'

No one was going to stop him. No fighter, no member of the crew. He was going to get this done.

Something changed, the noise, the feel through the controls. C-Charlie hesitated, slowed. What was happening? The engines? No, they were fine.

Then he knew what it was.

'Howard!' he yelled over the intercom. 'The bomb bay doors are open! Get them shut, now.'

The aircraft jumped up slightly.

'Corkscrew! Corkscrew!'

Douglas reacted immediately to Taylor's call, pulling the controls over and kicking the rudder.

Even over the roar of the engines he could hear the Browning's fire, and yellow light streaked over the canopy.

LMF 66

27/1/44 12.30 am

Roland felt the bomb bay doors open as he pulled back the curtain and stepped out into the nose. Why? It was too soon, they were still well short of the target.

Then he was thrown against the aircraft's side as the corkscrew started. Even as he braced himself though, he saw something in the baleful light of the burning town ahead that made him shout.

'Howard! What the hell are you doing?'

The bomb aimer's expression spoke eloquently of his guilt.

He had his hand on the bomb toggles and stared back at Roland in horror.

LMF 67

G erry was in a nightmare, one where awful things were happening but you were quite unable to do anything but go along with it.

He had his turret rotated to the rear where Adam had reported the stalking fighter. Now the attack had started and Dag had commenced the banking, diving and climbing man-oeuvre known as the corkscrew. He hadn't seen the fighter, only the streaks of tracer from it, but had fired into the dark-ness out of solidarity.

Now he had stopped firing. There was no point, in fact he was better not giving their position away.

His heart was pounding. The cannon shells had come close to Adam's turret, in fact they seemed to have passed through it. Was he alright? Oh please, God, let Adam be...yes! He was firing. He was still okay.

For now anyway. The fact he was firing meant the fighter was still in touch.

He worried for Adam but also for himself and the rest of the crew. What chance did they have against a fighter now it had found them? It was nimble, armed to the teeth, it could out manoeuvre and out range the lumbering Halifax, they had no chance, none, none, none.

He wanted to run, to get the hell out of there, bail out.

He fought it back, made himself stay. He wasn't going to let his crew down, not again.

LMF 68

27/1/44 12.31 am

Adam's heart was pounding even faster than the combined reports from the four Brownings he was firing into the blackness.

He had been lucky to see it. He'd been convinced the fighter would come from his right but, instead, he had caught a slight movement low and to his left. He'd been staring into the night so fiercely that his eyeballs felt like they were burning.

Burning, that was appropriate.

It had been the fires that had given him the break. Ahead of C-Charlie the town was glowing, reflected on the bank of clouds behind. The Junkers 88 had appeared like a dark cross silhouetted against them, an avenging angel of death rapidly closing for the kill.

But its shells had missed. They had come so close he'd heard them whip by like a swarm of angry wasps, but they had still missed. The fighter had followed them into the corkscrew but now the firing had stopped. When this registered, he forced himself to stop firing. No point in making it easier for the hunter to find them.

They were still alive. Sarah was not a widow yet.

But for how long?

LMF 69

27/1/44 12.31 am

'I can't see it anymore. We may have lost it. Stand by.'

'Good. Keep your eyes peeled.'

Howard only barely registered the messages over the intercom, that and the fact that the violent twisting of the corkscrew had stopped. All he could see was Saunders, stood over him.

'What are you doing?' Saunders demanded again, yelling to be heard over the noise. Howard jerked his hand off the bomb release controls. He had to think, had to say something.

'It just opened by itself,' he said. 'It must be faulty. I was trying to sort it.'

He could tell Saunders didn't believe him.

'Well, try them now. Get the doors closed.'

'They won't shut. It must be the hydraulics.'

'Let me try.'

'No, it's alright, I can man -'

But Saunders -ushed his hand aside and his own went straight to the bomb bay controls, moving them to the closed position. The noise of the airstream changed, signalling that the doors had responded.

'They seem to work fine,' said Saunders.

'Bomb aimer! What the fuck are you playing at?' The skipper's voice stung his ears.

'They didn't when I tried,' Howard said to Saunders. 'It has to be an intermittent fault. You know what this old crate's like, it's a wreck.'

Saunders just stared. Disbelieving, it was obvious.

'You dropped a bomb,' he said. 'I felt it go.'

'I...er...I was trying to get the doors shut. I must have....The controls, they're close together, you know, in the dark...'

Saunders shook his head and Howard knew why. It wasn't dark in the nose, the flames from the target illuminated virtually every detail of his workplace.

'Whatever,' he said. 'You've not fused the bombs, have you?'

'I...er,' he began, looking for an excuse. He couldn't find one. 'No, I haven't.'

'Bomb aimer! Answer, damn you!'

'Go and do it, quickly,' said Saunders. 'We're ten minutes from the target.'

'Right, yes. Er, does the skipper know?'

'Not yet.'

'Please. Don't tell him.'

Saunders had turned away. 'Just get it done, Howard,' he said, then, with one last look through the nose at the target, he headed up the steps towards the cockpit.

Howard swallowed. He'd been caught in the act, and by the skipper's best buddy. He seemed to know his way around the bomb aimers position too. He'd tell the skipper and then what was he going to do?

Well, he needed to fuse the bombs. And he'd better

placate that damned man.

He switched on his intercom.

'Sorry Skipper. I think there was a fault in the bomb circuits. It seems okay now.'

There was a significant pause before he got a reply.

'Right.'

That was it, a single word heavy laden with disbelief.

Howard retrieved his parachute pack and headed towards the bomb bay. He was not surprised to find Saunders stood next to the pilot.

He was careful not to look at them.

LMF 70

Roland saw Dag turn to watch Howard's indistinct fig-ure retreating into the gloom behind them, before turning to look forward again.

'Where's he going?' he yelled over the clamour.

Roland hesitated. Should he say? He had no reason not to now. He stepped up close to Dag's ear and unclipped his mask.

'To fuse the bombs. He'd forgotten,' he said.

Dag shook his head. 'Useless fucker,' he said. 'And you're as bad. You knew, didn't you? You knew he hadn't done it, but you didn't bother to tell me. Thanks for that.'

'There wasn't time. You were busy with the fighter.'

'Yeah, yeah, of course I was.' Dag stared straight ahead. 'Of course, that's not not the only thing you didn't bother to tell me about, is it?'

Roland took a deep breath of oxygen before removing his mask again.

'Dag, I'm sorry. We were -'

'I don't want to hear it.'

'Dag -'

'Fuck off! Understand?'

199

Dag's shout was so loud that Harrison flinched, hand on parachute, clearly thinking the fighter was back. Roland had had enough, he headed back to his position, giving the engineer a reassuring pat as he did.

He settled into his seat and closed the curtain behind him. He was trembling, chilled to the bone, but not just from sitting within the uninsulated metal box that was C-Charlie. He knew he had been shaken by the last few minutes, the fighter attack, finding Howard and knowing that the bomb aimers actions had been deliberate, that he was trying to sabotage their mission. That was enough but now it was worse because he had seen the expression on Dag's face.

It was a look that would forever haunt him. Every time he looked at Connie, he was sure he would see it, Dag's face bathed in a satanic red, his features distorted by rage, eyes flashing with pure anger, demented, unbalanced -

Roland stopped himself. Was that fair? Was Dag really unbalanced? He'd heard that talk, before he was injured but he'd never seen it himself. In the air, Dag was abrasive, single-minded, always had been but Roland had always felt he could trust him.

But then Connie had told him about the rages, the brooding, irrationality and near paranoia. Then his moods would swing; Dag could be funny, the life and soul of the party, outgoing, friendly, like more than one person lurked within him.

Then there was the 'incident' while Roland was in hospital, that had caused their old crew to refuse to ever fly with him again. It was after their last regular mission. That had been bad enough, but it had been sorted out with yet another new bomb aimer. No one outside the crew knew for certain exactly what had happened, they had refused to say even to the WinCo on the grounds that they feared he might be charged with something. There had been rumours though. Rumours about barrel rolling a Halifax on a training flight. Roland had dismissed them, they didn't sound like the Dag he knew, but then Connie had told him about the spells of euphoria, and he was no longer so sure.

He swallowed. This was a great place to start thinking about this, deep in enemy territory, on the run into the target. Now wasn't the time.

He plugged into the static oxygen point, stowed the personal bottle, then lugged his intercom back in.

' - the boozer's flashing again. Gunners, watch out.'

At least Dag was still on the ball. That was good news.

The bad news was that the fighter was back.

'Corkscrew! Corkscrew!'

LMF 71

Deja vu.

It was a repeating nightmare, one he couldn't wake from. Everything was unreal, the darkness, staring at shapes, scanning for movement, metal amidst the murk, for the killer in the clouds.

Then the realisation, the call as the cannon shells erupted from the night, rushing up towards him, vulnerable, as good as naked against the hot metal in his perspex bubble, helpless in his fragile human frame.

Human. A husband. A father - nearly anyway.

The vision of Sarah, abandoned at her hour of need.

'I'm doing my best,' he muttered as he pulled the trigger.

The hammering, pounding, skull rattling reports from the four Brownings, the smell of cordite, the g-force building as the Halifax banked and dived, it had all happened before.

But now there was a change. A bang. Flames. Were they hit?

The fighter dropped out of view, Adam rotated the turret to follow. Or tried to. Abruptly, the turret stopped moving.

This was no longer deja vu, this was a different nightmare. He was trapped, unable to move, unable to even escape, the rear door was fouled by the fuselage.

He hammered at the controls, cursing, whilst desperately searching for the fighter. Where was it? He was screwed, totally screwed. This was it, this was the end.

LMF 72

'**B**urt, Burt! Feather the port outer! It's blown, it's blown.'

Douglas, already committed to the corkscrew, had been caught unprepared by the engine failure, the sudden drag from the port wing as the Merlin turned in an instant from asset to handicap, tons of scrap iron with a rigid trefoil airbrake now rigid in the airstream. He had been banking to starboard, but the drag had tugged them straight and then to the left and now he was fighting for control, just at the point where they needed to manoeuvre.

They were a sitting duck, a fairground target, lit up by their burning engine.

'Burt, do something! Don't just stand there!'

LMF 73

Burning, falling, unable to move, unable to do anything, unable to change anything.

F-Freddie, Burt's home, his workplace, where he had his cobbers, was dying, disintegrating in an orgy of screams from tortured metal and terrified men. Flames, dancing, teasing, twisting flames, splintering into a million dots, dancing around him like fireflies.

Why didn't the shouting stop? It had before, why didn't it now? Make it stop, please make it stop, Mags, please make it stop.

LMF 74

27/1/44 12.36 am

Gerry was being battered.

This was not normal corkscrewing, C-Charlie was out of control, lurching, plunging, spinning. Had been since the port outer had erupted with an almighty bang and a shower of sparks.

He was sure it had not been hit by the fighter, it had just blown. So much for all that guff they'd been fed, about proper repairs, not to worry about the smoke; it was what he'd always suspected, a lie to get them in the air.

What a mess. The burning engine was leaving a comet trail of flames behind it. Why didn't they put it out, operate the extinguisher? The tanks would catch. They'd blow but, even before then the structure would weaken, the wing would break off. They'd have no chance, absolutely none, they'd be pinned by the violence of the spinning and tumbling of the disintegrating machine, their puny muscles unable to beat the laws of physics.

Bail out, bail out, he should go now!

But there'd been no call...but, there, someone had gone, he saw an object leave from the rear crew door and hang in space alongside them momentarily before vanishing.

Had there been a call from Dag? No, but what if the skipper was hit, was dead.

Gerry started to unfasten his harness.

'Roland! Get here and help me!'

The skipper. He *was* still there, C- Charlie was still diving, still aflame but was coming back under control. He should stay, protect the crew, protect Adam.

Adam! His turret hadn't moved, not for the last minute and it was cranked over in a position that jammed the rear door against the aircraft's structure. He couldn't get out like that. Was he hit? Was he dead? He couldn't be, no, no, no, Gerry told himself, he just wasn't firing so as not to give away their position.

But that was stupid, he was fooling himself. Their position was obvious, the burning engine could be seen for miles, anyone with eyes could see them, fighters, flak, searchlights. This was the end, oh God, oh God, oh God, he needed to get out.

Again he started to fumble with his belts but again he made himself stop. Stop being selfish, think of Adam, the rest of them. If Adam was dead he was their only defence. There had been no bail-out call, he had to stay, do his job. He wouldn't let anyone down again.

Forget the danger. Forget his fear. Look for the fighter. Not that he'd ever seen one, not for real.

There it was! He could see it. It was over to port, in the blind spot of the wing, illuminated by the flames. It was unbelievably close, too close. Had it misjudged their speed, their course? He could see every detail, the speckled camouflage, the antennae on the nose, the cockpit canopy, even the face of the pilot looking over at him.

Time stood still.

His turret was rotated towards the German machine, his guns almost in the perfect position, if only the fighter would rise or the wing fall -

As if on command, it rose into his sights. The fighter was trying to bank away, Gerry had a perfect view of its belly.

He fired.

Fireflies danced all over the Junkers. He couldn't miss, it seemed to Gerry that every bullet he fired hit the other aircraft. It glowed from within, like a Chinese lantern, before it fell away out of view.

He'd got it. That was a fatal hit. To his shame he found he was yelling in delight, punching the air.

Then the shame hit. He'd just killed people, men just like him.

Then he remembered Adam.

And the fire.

LMF 75

It was so quiet, peaceful even.

He couldn't enjoy it though. He'd been caught. Saunders knew what he'd done. And he'd obviously told the skipper, made it official. That was it, the end.

What would have happened if he'd managed to release all of the bombs? A court martial? No, probably not, it would have been done quietly, within the squadron but the results would have been very public. He'd have been damned with those dreadful letters: LMF. It would be stamped all over his file, his rank badges would be ripped off his uniform. The stain would have gone with him wherever he went, like a Roman slave branded on their foreheads for trying to escape.

Well he had escaped, and he would not be branded. He was not LMF, not a coward. It had taken courage to do this.

The cold was extreme, the frost biting his exposed cheeks and despite his gloves, his hands were numb. His eyes streamed, through the cold and tears of self-pity, and ice was forming painfully on his lids making blinking increasingly difficult.

Howard looked up, his canopy clearly visible in the glow of the burning city. The wind was blowing him away from Essen, away from the fires, that was a relief. Where would he land though? Would they treat him well? There were horror stories, crews beaten to death, lynched. it was too late now though, he couldn't go back. The reception surely could not be any worse than he'd have received back in Cambridgeshire. They wouldn't have understood that their pilot had been leading them to disaster, that he'd had to act.

There was the sound of firing up above, flames, the sound of screaming engines. That was it, C-Charlie had gone, the fighter had got them. Would any of them have got out? Would he see Saunders in captivity? That would be a disaster. Was it wrong to hope they were all dead? No, it was too bloody awkward if they weren't.

Wreckage, twisting and tumbling, fell past him. He was in danger! This wasn't fair, the Halifax was after him, intent on taking him with it.

But then a recognisable piece, illuminated in red, fell past him. Part of a wing.

With black crosses on it.

Not the Halifax. It was German.

An engine was screaming, tortured, uncontrolled, dying. Above him.

Getting closer.

LMF 76

'At some point, during the confusion of the fighter attack, the bomb aimer, p/o HOWARD, appears to have bailed out.'

27/1/44 12.37 am

'I got him! I got him! He's going down.'

Douglas registered the gunner's exultation, but he was still fighting C-Charlie, pulling the controls against the drag of the seized and still burning engine.

'Roland! Where are you?' he yelled into the intercom.

Someone grabbed his shoulder.

'I'm here, what can I do?'

'Feather the port outer, quickly!'

'But -'

'Just do it!'

Roland leant over the engine controls, but Douglas could not look away from the artificial horizon. He had to stop C-Charlie from spinning: with the drag from the propellor and the lack of engine power combined with their altitude, there would be no way he could recover it this time. He was keeping it from happening - just - by his own strength, by pulling the yoke to one side and standing on the starboard rudder pedal. His muscles were screaming, cramp forming in his right calf, but he would get no relief until -

Abruptly, C-Charlie lurched even more to port. He was losing it. They were going.

'Sorry!' Roland yelled above the clamour. The pressure eased again, returning to a fight he could just about win.

'What the fuck did you do?'

But then he felt the pressure ease further. The Halifax was not the most communicative of mounts, but he could feel the reduction in drag almost as if C-Charlie was a Spitfire. The relief on his body was like a glass of ice-cold water on a blistering summer's day.

They were not out of the woods yet though. They were still losing height and were still on fire.

'Extinguisher! Port outer.'

'Right, hold on.'

'Make sure you get the right one.'

'I will this time.'

This time? Douglas wondered about this for a moment then realised; Roland had feathered the wrong engine, albeit briefly. Was every idiot on this plane trying to kill him?

'Okay, I think I've got it.'

Douglas could now risk a glance. The engine was smoking but the flames were out.

'Yeah,' he said. Then he remembered to say, 'Thanks. Well done.'

'What's up with Harrison? Burt, are you okay?'

'Fuck knows, he just froze,' said Douglas. 'I was yelling at him for help, but he didn't bloody well move.'

Roland was shaking the engineer. 'Burt, what's wrong?'

'Just leave him. Actually, no, don't he's going to get in the way there.' He flicked his mic on. 'Hiley, get up here. I need you to look after the engineer.'

'Yes, sir.'

'Why can't I look after him?' said Roland.

'Because I need you up here. I'll need you in the run into the target.'

Douglas waited for the protest but, instead, another voice came on the intercom.

'Skipper. Rear gunner. I've got a problem.'

LMF 77

27/1/44 12.45 am

'But I keep telling you, the hydraulics have failed.'

'And I keep saying, the manual controls work, don't they?'

'Yes, but -'

'And your guns still work. They're only scarecrows anyway.'

There was a pause in the argument. John looked across at his roommate. Harrison was sitting on the floor near John's feet. He had allowed himself to be led from the cockpit and had meekly sat down when John had suggested it but had not said a word and was glassy-eyed with a blank expression. It was like he was totally bewildered, like he had woken from a dream and was unsure what was real.

Should he talk to him, try and bring him back? Was this like sleepwalking? People said that you shouldn't try to wake sleepwalkers, didn't they? That the shock could kill them.

He didn't want to kill Burt.

'Mid-upper gunner. My guns were more than scarecrows, Skip. I got that fighter, didn't I? Over.'

'Yes, and don't we know it. I'm sure you'll get your medal.'

There was another pause.

'I didn't do it for that, Skipper. I was protecting us.'

'You were doing your job, like all of us do - or should be doing. Our job is to bomb the target and that's what we're going to do.'

'But we can't go on with my turret like this.'

'Stop the chatter, stop moaning. We're going on.'

'We're too damned low and we've got an engine out.'

'ENOUGH! Be quiet!'

The intercom fell silent again. Was it always like this on ops? Not only the attacks, the flak, the problems with the aircraft but the crew at each other's throats? It didn't seem right.

He adjusted his radio, trying to improve the reception, forgetting his injured wrist. The bones grated together, bringing tears to his eyes. He guessed he wouldn't fly again until it healed. That would be hard, the longer he didn't fly the greater the dread would be, he needed to get back on the horse quickly.

He'd find out when they got back.

If they got back. They were far too low, so low they didn't need oxygen. Could they climb with three engines?

The engineer would know. They needed theirs. He glanced at Burt again. He had to try.

'Burt,' he said. 'You all right?'

Harrison showed no sign of having heard. Was there another way to get through to him?

'Burt, I've got some chocolate. I was going to have a piece. Would you like some?'

Nothing.

But he couldn't give up. He had to keep trying.

LMF 78

27/1/44 12.52 am

Roland had been talked through the instruments during training flights, months ago. Dag had wanted to prepare him for just such an eventuality as this, but that had been months ago, in daylight, with no pressure on him. This was very different: in darkness, deep over Germany, in trouble. Now they were just a meaningless collection of dials.

He also had another job to do. But who else was going to do this? Howard could after he'd dropped the bombs but, until then, he was needed. That left John, but he was very young, it would be hard on him on his first trip. So it had to be him, there was no one else.

Concentrate. What did he have to look at, what was important? Engine revs, which were the rev counters? He found them on Dag's panel, three pulling the same, one dead. Fine. To the engineer's panel. The top row were the cylinder head temps; again three looked fine. What was next? Oh yes, oil pressure and temperature. Two were the same but one, on the starboard inner, the readings were slightly lower on pressure and a bit higher on temperature. Was that important? Roland didn't know.

He did know that they couldn't afford to lose another engine. What height were they? He glanced back at Dag's panel; Seven thousand feet. Seven! They were gradually climbing but they should be at fifteen, sixteen thousand at least, the best this breed of Halifax could manage, which was feeble compared with the Lancs. The new Hercules engined Halifaxes with more power and extended wings could apparently do a lot better but that was no good to them now. They were too low, seven thousand was - actually, he couldn't bring himself to frame the right term, just that it wasn't enough.

Dag must know this, of course he did. He'd done 29 trips, he'd survived this long, he must be doing something right, so why was he being so bloody minded about this? Hell-bent on pressing on despite C-Charlie's long list of problems - the defective turret, a near catatonic engineer, a winged radio operator and a deeply unreliable bomb aimer.

Worst of all, though, was the loss of the engine. Every-one knew the Mk II Halifaxes were grossly underpowered even with four engines. Deleting the front turret had helped but they still had their bombload - well nearly all of it, thanks to Howard - they were going to struggle to maintain height, let alone climb.

Try to forget that. Being negative wasn't going to help anyone, not least himself.

Try to help. What else should he look at? Fuel, yes fuel. Something was nagging him about that, what was it? Oh yes, at some point they needed to switch from the outer wing tanks to the inners. When did it need to be done? He was pretty sure that on other trips to the Ruhr it had been done already. If it wasn't the engines would be starved of petrol, they'd lose them all, they'd crash. He found the fuel gauges, the needles were almost down to zero. It needed doing now.

The switch wasn't done from here though, the fuel cocks were back under the main spar. He'd need a torch to see in the dark, Harrison would have one, he'd have to get it off him.

He leaned over Dag, not wanting to use the intercom.

'I need to switch the tanks over. Won't be long,' he yelled.

Dag nodded, but then waved Roland back.

'Find that bloody useless bombardier too,' he said. 'We need him.'

Roland nodded and headed rearwards.

LMF 79

27/1/44 12.59 am

'Madness, this is utter madness.'

Adam kept muttering this as he used the manual handle to pump the turret around. It was slow, hard work, the only good thing about it was that it warmed him up. It was scant comfort. The worst thing about it all though was his impotence to do anything about it.

His memories of the turret stopping working and the nightfighter closing in on them flooded back. He had been utterly helpless, all sense and control driven from him in his panic.

He hadn't even thought to move the turret manually then, he had been too swamped by terror. His guns had been canted over to the left as the fighter came in directly behind them. He had been staring down the path of the cannon shells like he was travelling down a light-streaked tunnel. He had pressed himself back against his seat, trying to put a precious few inches of distance between himself and the deadly projectiles.

Then, even as this first ordeal ended, his fear, had continued. He'd thrown off his harness and hurled himself at the rear door of the turret, charging at it with his shoulder then scrabbling at it with his hands, sobbing, tears flowing down his cheeks, shouting, pleading for someone to come and save him.

And then, just as his fears subsided enough for the control - and the shame - to come back, the fighter was back, looming out of the darkness like an owl swooping on a helpless mouse. Again he'd been frozen, but now in acceptance of certain death.

Yet it hadn't fired. At the time he had the notion that it was toying with them, the owl had become a cat, playing with its prey, intensifying its enjoyment of the kill by exercising its power over the weak and defenceless. Now he knew it was probably because C-Charlies' flight had been so unpredictable that its course had taken the fighter by surprise and it was struggling to bring the Halifax back into its sights.

When Gerry's bullets had torn into its engines and cockpit, flames blossomed like chrysanthemums forming a wreath around the erstwhile predator, he had cried again, in relief this time.

It took minutes for the paralysis to wear off, but it left a bitter taste in his mouth and utter shame throughout his soul. Had anyone heard him? What would they think of him? He had apologised to the crew - but then found that his intercom had become disconnected. He hoped that had happened early on and no one had overheard his breakdown.

And still they went on. His mic was now working but to what end? He had protested but he had not been listened to.

As he scanned the night sky, C-Charlie rocked in the first bursts of flak from the Ruhr itself.

LMF 80

C - Charlie rocked and, even over the thrum of the three working Merlins and the air rushing over the aluminium skin and protuberances of the Halifax airframe, Roland could hear the crump of the flak bursts. That had to be the Ruhr defences. At least the guns meant less risk of fighters, but that was scant consolation; they were alone, too low and too slow. Every gun within range would be swinging towards them.

He couldn't think like that, he had to get on with his job, or at least the one that Dag had given him. Now that meant switching the fuel cocks over. The outer tanks were nearly dry, one of the engines coughed whilst he was getting the torch off the engineer's belt. Harrison was getting better, but he seemed to have no idea where he was or how he'd got there. Roland mentally crossed his fingers that he would recover enough to resume his duties, Roland still had to find them a route home.

Now he was literally working in the dark. He knew what to do in principle but it was daunting to do this for real. If he got it wrong, he'd starve the three remaining engines. If they lost just one more engine they'd be down. With some trepidation he opened what he hoped were the right fuel cocks and held his breath waiting for the engine notes to change.

All was good. The engines kept running.

He sighed with relief and got to his feet. He was about to return to the cockpit when a thought struck him; he hadn't seen Howard. He should be nearby fusing the bombs, well he should be done by now. Had he missed him when he was with John and Burt? It didn't seem possible.

He found an intercom point and plugged in, listening for a few seconds, not wanting to interrupt anything important but all was quiet.

'Dag, I've switched the tanks over. The engines should be drawing from the inners now.'

'Okay, yes that looks fine...fuck it!' C- Charlie trembled and bucked, flak reports booming through the fuselage. 'That was close. Get back up here, I'm going to need you.'

'Will do.' Roland hesitated and then switched his mic on again. 'Howard, are you back in the nose?' He waited. Nothing. 'Howard, where are you?'

'Howard, damn you, answer!' Dag's temper had flared again. 'Where the fuck is he? Find the useless sod.'

'Will do,' said Roland. 'He might be on the thunderbox.'

'Well, he's a complete shit so that's about right.'

Ease off, Dag, Roland thought, Howard may have his weaknesses but he was still one of the crew and he had feelings. Hopefully he was unplugged and hadn't heard.

He himself unplugged and headed back. Using Harrison's torch he ducked around Gerry's turret but then instantly knew something was wrong. It was colder and noisier in the rear part of the fuselage than it should have been, and he knew why. The crew door on the side of the machine was open and, shining the light towards the Elsan, it was obvious that no one was there.

He felt faint.

Howard was gone. He'd bailed out.

LMF 81

Douglas flinched as a triple burst of flak over the port side of the nose sent a series of sharp, metallic cracks through the airframe. He had to react quickly to hold C-Charlie steady, heading towards the mass of flames that was their target. They were still a way off, twelve minutes, perhaps fifteen.

But they were so close, so close. He could taste it, taste the end.

More flak burst around them, the entire sky lit up by flashes. Searchlights sprang up from the ground, single, vertical lights, joined then by others, swinging towards Douglas's aircraft. He knew the pattern; the radar-controlled master beam with the rest of the searchlight battery following its lead. C-Charlie would be on their screens, possibly the only return.

'No, you don't,' he muttered and edged them away.

He was tingling all over, not on edge but not...normal. All his senses were heightened, sensitised, he was not scared as such but jumpy and nervous, there was no doubt of that but there was something else; he felt alive. Alive and vital. Strange at a time when he could die at any moment that he should feel like this, but it was always the same. How could he stop doing this? Over the last months, on the nights when the squadron had flown but he hadn't, he'd felt bereft, lost, cheated, emasculated even. Missions were like air, he needed them to breathe.

He couldn't stay though. Not now. He'd burned too many bridges. The Wingco didn't want him, he didn't get on with many in the sergeants' mess nor with any of the officers, to be honest. And now there was -

Another master searchlight appeared directly ahead. Douglas kicked the rudder bar and then applied some bank with the yoke. The aircraft trembled as it bumped through flak disturbed air, would the searchlight follow, find them? No, the night remained dark. They'd escaped, no HE had escaped because he was good at this. Yes, they had lost a little more of their precious height, but it made little difference whether they bombed at 8000 or 7800. At least at that height their useless bomb aimer had a chance of hitting the target.

He was too good to stop doing this. He couldn't do a desk job and training. No thanks. So he'd leave but apply for another tour, have a break - a short break - yes, but come back to this. But somewhere else.

Away from here where his best friend and the woman he loved had betrayed him.

Perhaps he could get on Mosquitos. Fast, glamorous and only one other person to deal with, the navigator.

And, speaking of the devil, Roland was back. He leant in close.

'What?' yelled Douglas. He hoped this was important, he didn't want to hear more whinging.

'Dag, I've got some bad news,' said Roland.

LMF 82

'The remaining crew continued towards the target.'

27/1/44 1.11 am

'**S**hane, what you doing here, boy? Strewth, you're a sight for sore eyes.'

John was listening to a message on his headset so did not react to Burt's words. Then he had no choice, his bad arm was seized, and he was tugged round to face the engineer.

'Shane! Don't ignore your old man.'

John winced. The bones in his wrist grated. 'Burt, I'm not Shane. I don't know who Shane is, please let go,' he said.

Harrison leaned closer, blinking, the only illumination being the dim lamp on John's radio table.

'You're not Shane?' he said.

'No Burt, I'm John, John Hiley.'

Burt stared at him, then slowly nodded. 'John. Oh yeah, you've just arrived, haven't you?' He let go of John's arm.

'Yes, that's right. We're roommates.'

Burt nodded again. He reached into his Sidcot suit and took a silver hip flask out. He undid it, took a drink then offered it to John.

'No thanks, Burt.'

'Yeah, probably right. We're going to be flying later.

Need to keep a clear head. Good lad.'

C-Charlie shuddered and bumped as another flak salvo burst nearby. The noise and vibration was constant. How did Burt not know that they *were* flying? Still, he thought it best to humour the Australian.

'Yes, that's right, Burt. Because we'll be flying,' he said.

Burt took another swig. He looked thoughtful. 'Keeps the cold out though. Bleedin' country's so damn cold. Wet too. Don't know how you Poms put up with it.'

John adjusted his dials, trying to get a clearer signal on the VHF. A message was being transmitted from the Master Bomber. It was on the way home. He'd have to tell the skipper. The rest of the crew would hear though. They wouldn't be happy.

'Shane's my son,' said Burt. 'My eldest lad. I've got two, and two girls, but Shane's about your age. That's why I thought -' The crump of shells interrupted him. Burt looked puzzled. 'Who's bangin?' he said.

'Don't worry about it, Burt,' said John, writing in his log. 'Four, eh? Must keep you and your wife busy.'

'Busy? Well, Mags is. She runs the house. Well she did.'

'Did?'

'Yeah, she's crook. Really crook.'

'Crook?'

'Sick. Cancer.'

'Oh. I'm sorry.'

'She's dying, lad. That's why I need to do this last trip. One last trip then I can go home, that's what the wingco said.' Burt took another swig. 'One last trip,' Burt murmured.

Dying, thought John. That explained a lot. No wonder he seemed so distant, so distracted.

Which he was just now, he'd been distracted from his job. He switched on his intercom.

'Skipper, message from the Master Bomber. He's heading back.'

There was a long pause before he got a reply.

'Roger.'

That was it. John waited for the reaction from the rest of the crew.

To his surprise though, it was Burt who reacted.

'The Master Bomber?' he said. 'We're...we're...on a raid! What am I doin' back here? The skipper'll need me.'

And then he was gone, heading forward.

LMF 83

27/1/44 1.14 am

O f all the parts of a raid, Gerry hated this the most.

The only good thing about it was that the risk from nightfighters was minimal but only because the other dangers were at their highest. The route to the target tried to bypass the guns, but now they had to cross them to get to the target. He and Adam could do nothing to defend the aircraft, they were just passengers and -

A flash took his night vision. It was accompanied by a sharp crack shook him from his reverie but confirmed his fears at the same time. This was awful, the Ruhr was bad enough at the best of times but now, when they were just about the only thing in the sky, it was bloody terrible.

He was surprised Adam hadn't said anything about the Master Bomber heading home. That should have marked the end of the raid, the Master Bomber was normally the last one to leave. But still C-Charlie ploughed on.

Gerry swung his turret round to face forward, the air-flow note changing as the canopy moved through different angles. The whistling from the hole made by the flak hit was constant but the cold draft increased as the air rushing back over the cockpit poured through the gaps around the guns.

His night vision was slowly returning but the truth was the fires were so bright from the target that he didn't need it back completely. It was a scene from hell ahead, a mass of flames bathing the heavens in a menacing shade. With the fires on the ground reflected on the massed clouds above, it appeared like they were flying into a dark, gaping mouth that was eager to swallow them.

How long before they bombed? Ten minutes? Twelve?

He turned his turret around, not wanting to see any more.

But then he saw something worse. A Lanc, above them, caught in a searchlight. He watched it start to twist and bank, perhaps it could get - no, another beam had caught them, and two more. They were coned, there was no escape now. The deadly flowers were already blooming around the Lancaster.

He flicked on his intercom.

'Some poor sod's getting it above us,' he said.

'It's the Master Bomber.'

That was John. He'd be listening to the VHF.

'At least it's not us.'

The skipper, as sympathetic as ever. But he had voiced what Gerry, himself, was thinking.

He didn't want to watch but couldn't look away. He didn't want to watch other men die but that was what he was doing. The Lancaster was already on fire but then the end came brutally quickly. In a flurry of flak bursts the aircraft changed from something recognisable into a thousand flaming fragments falling to earth.

'Christ, the poor bastards.'

That was Adam. He didn't say anything more but what was left unsaid was more significant. The Master Bomber had been at the correct altitude, it had been undamaged, with all four engines. C- Charlie was low, slow and alone. But still going stubbornly onwards.

Then, suddenly, they weren't. They were banking,

turning away from the target.

Adam in the rear turret had noticed too. 'What's going on? Are we going home?'

The Skipper replied almost immediately.

'Crew, stand by and watch out for fighters.'

'What's happening?'

'We're just sorting out a problem up here. Out.'

'Another one?' said Adam. 'What now? Why aren't we going home?'

There was no reply.

LMF 84

27/1/44 1.20 am

'What the hell are we doing? This is bloody crazy!'

'Keep off the mic unless you need to call something in.'

'What, until we find the fighter that's going to finish us off?' Roland could hear the anger in Adam's voice. 'Madness! We're circling, we're actually circling over Germany. For fuck's sake, I don't care what the issue is, drop the bastard bombs and let's get the hell back to England.'

'I've told you, keep quiet. You do your job and I'll do mine.'

'How can I do my job when my turret doesn't blasted well work?'

'Out!'

Dag shook his head, then gestured Roland closer. 'Come on,' he shouted over the clamour. 'Roland, you've got to do this.'

Roland glanced across at Burt who had reappeared a few minutes before. 'I don't know,' he yelled into the pilot's ear. 'I think you need me up here.'

Dag shook his head vigorously. 'No, I don't. Harrison's fine now. He's doing his job again.'

That's wishful thinking, Roland thought. Burt had

clearly had some kind of mental collapse. Could he really recover that quickly? But he also knew he was hanging his reluctance to do what Dag had asked him on the engineer's fitness when the truth was the problem lay with Roland himself.

He leaned in towards Dag's ear again. 'Adam's right. We should dump the bombs and head home.'

'No!' yelled Dag. 'No, no, no!' His voice was so loud that Burt glanced over at the pair. Even over the tremendous racket in the cockpit, he'd heard the pilot shout.

'Calm down, Dag,' Roland said.

'No, I won't calm down. If we abort the whole bloody trip won't count, we'll have to do it all over again. *I'll* have to do it all over again.'

'Yes, but...'

'You want rid of me, you and Connie. This way you get shut of me tomorrow.'

'That's not...'

'Yes, it is and I don't care anymore. You two can do what you like, I don't give a damn. All I care about is getting this done and getting the hell out of here. And to do that I need you.'

Roland stared out through the windscreen. This was surreal. He and Connie had discussed how they'd tell Dag about their relationship, talking about it at 7,000 feet whilst circling over Germany in a handicapped aircraft with no bomb aimer was not something that had occurred to them. And he was being blackmailed, pure and simple, blackmailed with the crew being held to ransom, every second they spent here exponentially increasing the risk of being intercepted by a fighter. The pressure on him was sickening.

'You're a trained bomb aimer,' said Dag.

'I didn't graduate.'

'Yes, but that was your choice. You finished the course, didn't you?'

'Yes, but...'

'Yes but you needed to be able to hide, to lie to yourself, didn't you?'

Roland didn't reply.

'The lying's over, Roland,' shouted Dag. 'You know that we've all killed. You, me, our gunners, the radiomen, whoever, we're all in this together. We're all killers.'

Roland's head dropped.

'You need me to navigate a course for the route back,' he said.

'I need a bomb aimer *now*. And Taylor is right about one thing. The more we piss about around here, the more chance we'll get picked off anyway. Either we die or some of them do. It's down to you, Roland. Your choice.'

LMF 85

'Other minor technical problems with the aircraft were encountered.'

27/1/44 1.26 am

Adam thumped the breeches of his guns repeatedly with his gloved fists.

Too low, too slow, one engine down. They should be running for the coast but, instead, what were they doing? Circling, they were actually bloody circling, away from the worst of the flak, sure, but in the nightfighter zone. What a tempting target they were, a fat, wounded bird pregnant with iron eggs, waddling around the sky. His turret was barely functioning either. He might as well hang a sign off his guns; 'Please feel free to shoot us down'.

And no one was listening. They were in the hands of a madman. Dag - what kind of nickname was Dag anyway? A pretentious one. A sergeant with a double-barrelled name, wasn't that enough to tell anyone there was something wrong with the man, that he'd have an almighty great chip on his shoulder?

It was too bloody late to have these thoughts, wasn't it? Never again though, never again would he put his life in the hands of someone he didn't know or had the slightest doubts about.

If they got back.

If.

He thumped his guns again. They were so bloody helpless.

Why was he the only one speaking up about it? Gerry was supposed to be his friend, one who owed him too, why hadn't he said anything? This wasn't a proper crew, was it? A proper crew would pull for each other, care enough about each other not to take risks like this. Now none of them even had the courage to say a word, no one was backing him up. He was always cold and isolated in any aircraft but now his isolation had been made total by everyone else's silence.

Cowards, the bloody lot of them.

'The bombs are fuzed, Dag. He did that.'

Whose voice was that? Saunders, the navigator. The pilot's best buddy. What was he doing checking the bombs? Was that the problem?

'Right. Crew, we're turning back to the target again. Skipper out.'

No, no, no! Madness, utter madness. But what was the point in him saying anything? No one would back him up. Why was he the only sane one? Didn't they care about their lives?

Something bothered him about about what Saunders had said. 'He did that.' He, past tense. Had something happened to Howard?

None of his concern. He just needed to stay alive, to get back to Sarah and their new child.

He pumped the turret around manually. At least the physical activity warmed him up.

It was scant consolation.

LMF 86

There was a strange smell in the bomb aimer's position, sour and yeasty, which Roland couldn't place.

It was the least of his worries.

He shouldn't be doing this. It had been hard enough simply to join up, he'd wrestled with his conscience, alone, before he'd decided that the greater good was served by taking up arms against evil.

But his limits had been exposed in training.

Even when it was just pretend, the simple act of pressing the bomb release button had been too much. Too much of everything. Too much imagination, too much empathy, too much humanity - was it possible to have too much of that in a world that was tearing itself apart? Whatever, he couldn't do it.

But now he was going to have to. He was going to drop bombs on people - men, women and children, the elderly and infirm. The old nightmares came back; of the blast that could rip the lungs out of those nearby, the white-hot shrapnel that tore bodies apart, decapitated and eviscerated. Or, if it didn't kill them straight away, buried people alive, suffocated and crushed them. But they were also carrying incendiaries, and they, if anything were worse: the foul chemicals within would not stop burning whatever they fell on, brick, tile, timber, cotton or flesh.

Horrible, just horrible.

And he was going to do it.

But Dag was right, he had been lying to himself being a navigator, telling himself he was just guiding the crew there and then getting them back when really he was the man driving the hired killers to the contract, helping them set babies alight.

He always had been.

So, in truth this was not such a big step. Lying on his stomach, looking through the bombsight whilst C-Charlie bored in towards the target at 160 knots, readying himself to deliver an almost complete bomb load onto an already burning city and a tortured and terrified population was only a small step from what he'd been doing before.

No.

He was lying to himself again.

It was a huge step. He was going to kill.

He felt sick.

It came to him what the smell was.

LMF 87

G erry felt cheated. It wasn't fair, he'd made his first kill then had the hope that they were turning back. He'd pictured himself being able to celebrate his victory with Adam and bask in the glow of admiration.

He'd be alive too but that, didn't seem the most important thing, it was the unfairness that got to him. He'd done his bit, stayed at his post, fought off the fighter. Now he'd never get the credit.

Because, whatever new problem they'd had they'd resolved. They'd turned back. And now they were going to get shot down. The flak had started up again, it was like Dag was saying to the gunners 'you missed the first time, but I'll give you another go'. It was odds on that they'd be hit; they were coming in at exactly the same height.

Madness.

Unfair.

As if to confirm his thoughts, a barrage of shells burst exactly at their level, close enough to rock them and be heard over the clamour. Gerry could hardly breathe, that was so close, it might have been something as small as the slightest gust of wind that had deflected the missiles away from them. He thought of the Master Bomber, of its end.

At least it was quick. Make it quick.

In the light of the target he saw the rudders deflect and felt the aircraft descend a little. That was good, at least the pilot was trying.

'Where's Howard?'

It took a few moments for the oddness of the question to get past Gerry's terror. That was Adam. Why was he asking that?

'I said, where's Howard? Damn well answer me.'

'Quiet! We're on the run into the target.'

The Skipper, furious.

'I want to know where he is. Why was Saunders checking the fuses and not Howard?'

'Shut up, Taylor.'

Gerry frowned. Adam was right, that had been an odd message from Roland. Howard should have done the job. Was he wounded, dead? Was that the problem that had caused them to circle?

But no, it wasn't that, was it? Suddenly Gerry had worked it out. That object he thought had fallen off the aircraft, he knew what it was.

He pressed his intercom button.

'He bailed out,' he said. 'I saw him go.'

LMF 88

'Is that true? Gerry, if you saw that why didn't you say anything?'

'Shut up, stop the chatter.'

'I hadn't realised what it was at the time. And I was busy with the fighter.'

Douglas wanted to scream at them, but he was fighting to keep control of C-Charlie. It was shuddering, rocking through the air churned by the flak bursts. It was like driving over a ploughed field, several times the controls had almost been ripped from his grip. He was trying to anticipate what the gunners were doing, constantly shifting their course and height. It was hard - and now this.

'That was ages ago.'

'Yes but…'

'Shut up, shut up, all of you, that's an order,' he yelled. 'I'm trying to keep you all alive here.'

'You're trying to kill us all, more like.'

'I've given you an order.'

'I think you'll find I outrank you.' That was Taylor.

'Not in the air you don't. What I say -'

C-Charlie was lifted by something big going off beneath its port wing. He thought he was going to lose her, but he caught the spin before it happened. By the time they were on an even keel again Roland was already speaking.

'Chaps, that's enough. This isn't the time. The skipper's got his hands full.'

'Saunders tell us the truth. What's going on?'

Douglas didn't have time to stop him.

'Okay, yes, it's true. Howard *did* bail out during the fighter attack. I've taken over.'

'But...you're the navigator. If anything happens to you, how do we get back?'

'I can be hit wherever I am, you know that.'

There was silence for a few seconds. Douglas felt it was time for him to say something.

'So now you know. Let's get this over and done with and get home.'

'But -'

'Enough!'

The silence on the intercom returned but now there was a sullenness about it. Well, let them sulk, let them hate him. In ten minutes - less - it would be done and -

Abruptly, everything turned a dazzling, painful white.

LMF 89

27/1/44 1.45 am

T he light thumped into Roland's eyes and brain with the force of a sledgehammer.

He twisted away from the perspex, into the darkness of the nose but, even with his eyes screwed tightly shut, he could still see the vivid orange skeleton image of the inside of the bombsight he'd been looking through seared onto his retina.

The light was like a physical assault. It drove all sense from him, all rational thought. His life was ending in confusion, oblivion starkly lit.

LMF 90

27/1/44 1.45 am

John gripped the edge of his radio table, despite the pain from his wrist.

Where was the light coming from? It seemed to be everywhere and nowhere. They weren't on fire, there was no heat, but there was noise, screams, concussions, huge thumps that seemed to grab and shake the aircraft like a rabbit caught in a terrier's jaws, their machine already twisting and diving.

Shattering, terrifying, his heart threatened to tear itself from his chest.

How much more? How much more?

LMF 91

S o this was how it ended.

Gerry had always loved being on the stage, in the spotlight, so it seemed apt that his final performance, his final act, should be in the criss-cross of searchlights. He was almost inclined to take a bow.

How many had coned them? Two, three? The skipper was banking, twisting, turning C-Charlie, trying to break free but it was hopeless.

Jump, Gerry told himself, jump, get out, save yourself, this was the end. The shells were getting closer, how had they not been hit? It could only be a matter of moments.

But he stayed, it was illogical, he knew, but it still felt infinitely safer to stay within the thin metal and plastic walls of their aircraft rather than launch his body, unprotected, out into the night.

He waited for the end, wishing, praying it would be quick.

Then the lights went out.

LMF 92

Douglas laughed, he was actually laughing. How lucky was that?

It had been hopeless, he'd been maneuvering blindly, instinctively, trying to break free of the lights but knowing it was impossible. The Halifax was just too slow, too clumsy at the best of times but, in their current state, didn't have the power to do much more than wallow about like a cow mired in deep mud.

Then they'd flown into the cloud.

It had suddenly gone dark, he was plunged into blackness, couldn't even see the instruments. He thought he'd gone blind, he panicked but then realised that the searchlights had taken his night vision, it would come back in time.

But they didn't have time, he had to react, use his other senses to save them, stop the lights finding them again. He turned C-Charlie, gently though, so they'd not lose height, not lose their precious cover. They weren't safe, far from it, the gunners seemed affronted by the loss of their quarry and had redoubled their efforts to bring them down. They would be following them by sound, he still had to keep turning, jinking, but carefully so as not to drop out of their moisture saviour.

He began a second turn, his vision beginning to recover.

An orange flash.

A bang.

Something thumped him hard - very hard - into the armour plate behind his seat. The force drove the breath from his body, he gasped, held onto the controls more for support than anything else but instinctively moved them. He was surprised to find they still worked. For a long few seconds he fought to breathe. Gradually he was able to.

Okay, get through the next few minutes. Then get home. It would be over.

All over.

He became conscious of a a bump in his metal seat behind his back. It was painful to rub against, his body was probably bruised, but, he found, it acted like a stimulant, keeping him sharp. He pushed back against the lump.

His night vision was really coming back now. They were still flying, they were through this. They'd survived.

They were so close to the target. If he turned back now it would all have been for nothing. The lump pushed into his back. It showed the armour plate had done its job.

As should he.

They were in the clear, the lights had lost them, the guns were now firing nowhere near them.

He turned them back towards the target. He'd get this done and then the lot of them could sod off.

He looked for Burt and found him, cowering, on the floor.

'Burt, Burt, get up, get up man.'

He didn't move. Douglas reached out and grabbed him.

'Come on, check the instruments. Check we're okay.'

This seemed to galvanize him into action.

Douglas pressed the intercom button. 'Crew, we're starting the bomb run. Be ready. Over.'

LMF 93

'The bomb run commenced slightly before 0200 with F/L SAUN-DERS acting as the bomb aimer.'

27/1/44 1.46 am

'Madness. Utter bloody madness.'

Roland wasn't sure who had spoken, Adam or Gerry, probably the former. It didn't matter, he agreed with them.

They had gone through so much but being coned by the searchlights had been shattering. They had been so helpless, a cockroach on the kitchen floor trying to avoid the boot that would crush them. There had seemed to be no escape.

But then, the miracle, they were free, alive. They had been given this gift, this deliverance. Surely, they should accept it, not throw it back. Dag had though, he was gambling.

'Keep your opinions to yourself. We're through the worst of the flak.'

Were they? He supposed Dag had a point, it <u>was</u> quieter. They might as well go on now. But still though, did Dag have a deathwish? He couldn't get the thought out of his head. Well, if he did, Roland had played a part in creating it. He had taken Connie from him, removed one of Douglas's main reasons for living. Sure, neither he or Connie had done it deliberately, they hadn't meant to fall in love with each other.

But he owed Dag. He should support him.

He flicked on his intercom.

'Dag's right. We've done the hard bit. We might as well go on now.'

There was silence.

Roland wished someone would say something, even if it was a put down because the silence on the intercom felt like condemnation. In supporting Dag he'd betrayed the others.

He swallowed his guilt down and tried to get on with the job.

However, as soon as he looked through the bombsight, he realised that there was a problem.

He switched on the intercom again.

'Dag, Roland here. The cloud cover's complete. I've got no clear view of the target.'

'Just drop them through the clouds.'

That was Adam again.

'We haven't got H_2S, Adam.'

Gerry this time.

'Sod that. Just drop the bastards.'

'Quiet!' Dag's voice was authoritative. 'Roland, I'll reduce height until we drop out of it.'

This time the reaction was immediate, very vocal and, once again, Roland was in complete agreement with it.

LMF 94

Douglas's headphones were filled with shouts of protest.

'No! You can't do that! We can't go any lower.'

'We can't climb. We'd be shedding height we can't get back.'

It was both gunners now, not just Taylor. It felt like a mutiny. Well, sod them, he was in charge, it was his decision. He needn't say anything, but he switched his mic on anyway.

'It's the only way we're going to bomb, we need to see the target. And we'll be able to climb once we've dropped the load.'

'Then drop them now and let's get gone.'

'We don't need to see anyway. It's obvious from the fires when we're over the target.'

Ignore them, Douglas said to himself. Just ignore them.

But he switched the mic button.

'We need to see the target for the photoflash,' he said. 'If we don't then this trip won't count.'

'And there it is in a nutshell, isn't it?' Even over the clamour and bumps that was the interior of C-Charlie, the bitterness in Taylor's voice was obvious. 'It's all about you.

About you completing your tour. The rest of us don't matter. We don't have a say, do we?'

Douglas stared ahead impassively, automatically correcting C-Charlie as it bumped and rocked in the overheated air.

'Well?' demanded Taylor. 'That's right, isn't it?'

'Yes,' said Douglas, and pushed the control column forward.

LMF 95

'You madman, you fucking madman, you're going to kill us all.'

Roland felt sick, and it wasn't just from the drop in height.

'You might not have anything to live for but the rest of us do.'

'Be quiet.'

'No, I won't. I've got a baby coming that's going to be fatherless, just because you've got a chip on your shoulder. What is it, couldn't measure up to your old man?'

'Leave my bloody father out of it!'

'Adam, leave it.' That was Gerry.

'I won't leave it. He's a complete ass, everyone knows it, but we've got to suffer because of it. He doesn't care. He doesn't care about you, he doesn't care about Harrison. He's got four kids and a sick wife, did you know that, Skipper? Well, did you?'

Roland shook his head. He didn't know that either. It explained a lot.

But, before Dag could reply, their world changed. C-Charlie came out of the clouds.

They were over the city, it was more than burning, it was an inferno. And, at this height, it was obvious this was not a military target, this was the residential part. This was creepback realised, crews dropping the bombs early so they could get the hell out of it and home.

He could see why. They were at, what, 5000 feet? He could see everything, suddenly, and in complete clarity. It was overwhelming.

'Just drop the bastard bombs, Saunders.'

The anger had gone out of Taylor's voice. Even over the intercom, Roland could hear the shock and anguish. The vision was clearly getting to him too.

But then, it was more than just what he saw, all of his senses were experiencing the burning city. It would be the same for the rest of the crew as well.

His face was uncomfortably warm like he was sat too close to the hearth at home. The heat radiated through the Perspex, the metal skin of the aircraft was hot to the touch. Even over the roar of the engines, the rush of air, the vibrations, he could hear the crackle of the fire and the crash as buildings collapsed. C-Charlie bumped and tossed in the superheated air. The stench was awful, smoke, chemicals; the smell of burned meat told its own story of what things were like beneath.

But there was one thing that was worse than that: he could taste it. Burnt human flesh and the fabric and content of their destroyed homes sat on his tongue. As he swallowed, he took it down inside him.

It was like he was eating the city.

'Drop them, just drop the bastards! Please!'

'Shut up! Everyone but Roland.' Dag's voice cut through the fog. 'Roland, get the doors open and guide me in.'

The bomb doors. He'd forgotten to open them. What an idiot. He found the controls, swung the lever to open.

He stared through the perspex. 'What...where do I

drop them?' he said. 'There are no markers.'

'For God's sake, Roland, the marshalling yards, beyond the city centre.'

He settled to the sight. It was the one he was used to, largely automatic, the operator having to dial in four settings, two already set before the mission. The only settings that needed to be adjusted in flight were the measured wind direction and speed. He didn't know them, so he guessed. Surely that would do?

He looked through the sight, then wished he hadn't. Everything was crystal clear, houses consumed by flames, lives being destroyed. Then C-Charlie leapt and plunged as Dag fought for control in the tortured air and, momentarily, the images blurred. His relief didn't last long, they came back, in even greater clarity.

Concentrate, he told himself, do the job.

This wasn't his job though. And this was precisely why, these were very circumstances that he'd dwelt on, why he'd asked to be taken off the bomb aimer's course.

Stop it. It would be alright if they could hit the military targets. And at this height he could surely find them - yes, there they were. This was alright, he could do this.

'Right, right, right,' he said over the intercom.

'For pity's sake drop them!'

'Shut up!'

The aircraft's course adjusted. He was in control, he was now in command.

Him. No one else now.

'Left a little. Yes, that's it, leave it there.'

He was doing the job now. The training came back. He had regained control, he was dispassionate, detached.

'Steady, steady.'

His fingers closed over the bomb release mechanism.

He did not press it. He could see something through the optics of the bombsight, quite clearly.

There were people, fighting the fires, helping the wounded, rescuing. People like him, like his father, brother, like Connie, like all of them. People with hopes and dreams, people who'd done no harm to him, children of God.

The city below him was utterly devastated, smashed, broken, yet he was about to drop more misery on it.

He held the bomb release button. He knew he should press it. But he hesitated. This couldn't be right...could it?

LMF 96

27/1/44 1.53 am

'I can't. I can't do it.'

The meaning of the words took a few seconds to sink in for John, and apparently, it did with everyone else as there was silence on the intercom for a few seconds. Then everyone tried to speak at once, resulting in a squark of noise.

'That's enough, all of you!'

'Don't tell me to shut up you arrogant little -'

'QUIET!'

The Skipper's shout made John's ears ring.

'What do you mean you can't do it, Roland? Why not?'

'There are people down there.'

'Of course there are people. That's the enemy.'

'I know but...I can see them.'

'Just drop them, please.'

That was Gerry.

'Damn it, don't. It's too late, I'm taking her round again.'

John felt the G-force rise as the aircraft banked around.

'No, no, not again, please no,' said Gerry again.

'Saunders, damn you, just drop the bombs anywhere and get us the hell out of here.'

'Keep out of it, Taylor,' yelled the Skipper. 'Roland, don't you damn well touch that button until we're over -'

'Watch out! Flak tower!'

John felt something strike the aircraft.

'Suppression fire!'

Even as the the skipper spoke, John heard and felt Gerry fire. Moments later Adam, in the crippled rear turret, also opened up.

There was a huge bang. 'Christ this is hot,' someone said.

'Right, we're clear,' said the Skipper. 'Get ready to go around again.'

'No! No, you reckless bastard!'

'Quiet, Taylor. Roland? Roland, damn you, answer me.'

'I can't do it, Dag, please, I just can't.'

'Don't give me that Quaker claptrap, you joined up, you must do this. We're here to destroy the target.'

'The target IS destroyed. It's all gone. What difference will our bombs make? It's just not right.'

'Not right? The Nazi's brought this on themselves when they bombed our cities. What gives you the right to have morals? You know you put anything that stays your hands away when you sign up and it gets properly serious when you climb inside this aircraft. You know that, don't you?'

'Yes,' muttered Saunders.

'So you'll do what I bloody well tell you to do. When you get back you can decide what to do in the future, you and that duplicitous little bitch who's waiting for you. You make a fine couple. Now get ready to bomb.'

There was a brief pause. Then Roland replied; 'Okay, I'm ready.'

The intercom fell silent. Then someone, probably Taylor, said one word.

'Fuck.'

It did seem to sum it all up.

Morals, the luxury of morals. There were no other aircraft about, John had little to do at that moment but think.

He thought of something his father had once said to him: 'Morals, my son, are all about doing the right thing, not the easiest thing. Standing up for what you know is right and not being swayed by others into doing wrong.'

He could picture his father staring intently at him through his small, metal-framed glasses. 'If you follow these simple rules, your mother and I will always be proud of you.'

Would they be proud of him now? Not for his own actions but in their omission, in not standing up for Saunders. He was alone, friendless. If good people did not stand up for what they believed or supported others for what was right, then evil would triumph. This war, the Nazi regime, was all the proof anyone should need.

He reached for the intercom.

Still, though, he hesitated.

LMF 97

L ines of tracer arced up towards them, seemingly slow and lazy at first but then flashing by. Some, presumably small calibre and nearly spent, hit them.

Was it wrong to want to be hit by something larger? Of course it was, but Roland then, at least, would not have to go through with this. The cup would pass from his lips, he would not have to sip from the poisoned chalice, a drink that would undermine everything he believed in.

But Dag was right, he had been fooling himself. He had told himself that being a navigator was all right, that he was just helping the others to find their way to a point in Germany and then find their way safely home, that he was a guide not a killer. It was a lie, a comforting lie. They were all in it together, a collective, an instrument of war. Together they delivered death.

Some 500 men had already done what he was doing tonight, laying on their bellies, looking through the sights and delivering their aircraft's deadly loads onto the people below. They had done it, why should he be different? As Dag had said, why had he allowed himself the luxury of morals?

Because he had them, that was why. He lived by a code, he had understood what was right and what was wrong. The other bomb aimers had all bombed earlier, when the target was intact but this was like arriving when a fight was over and kicking people who were laying on the ground. It was cowardly. It was wrong.

The target came into sight again. This was it. He had to do it this time.

But how could he face his brother and father after this? How could he look Connie in the eye? She knew the dilemma he faced, had gone through the soul-searching, understood the compromise he'd reached with himself. He thought that Dag did too.

'Right, here we go again.' Dag's voice came over the intercom. 'Roland, you're going to do it this time, aren't you?'

It was more demand than question.

Before he could reply, others joined in.

'Please, Roland, just drop them,' said Gerry.

'Yes, just bloody well do it. We're over the city, just unload them. Sod your bloody beliefs, just do it! You're going to kill us.'

'Don't be hard on him, Adam,' said Gerry. 'It's tough for him.'

'It's hard for the rest of us too, what makes him so different?'

'Quiet, you two,' said Dag. 'Roland, over to you. Aim for the target.'

The intercom fell silent. It was just him now, him and the burning city, the people battling the fires that he could see through his bombsight.

Him and the bomb release button.

Him and his conscience, The soul he was about to taint forever.

He had to blink the tears away, it was hard to see.

He forced his mouth to work. 'Left,' he croaked. 'Left, left, steady.'

'It's different because he knows right from wrong.'

LMF 98

27/1/44 1.57 am

Who had spoken? Douglas wasn't sure, in fact he wondered whether he'd imagined it and created the words in his own head. But someone had said it – John?

He knows right from wrong.

That was true, it was one of the things that he liked about Roland, that had brought them close together in the first place. He was moral, certain, loyal.

But where did what he and Connie had done fit into that? It was bewildering.

'Right a bit, right, right.'

Automatically, Douglas reacted to Roland's instructions. C-Charlie was wandering as it bumped through the flame disturbed air.

In all the time that Douglas had known Roland he had only done something if he knew it to be right. That was why he'd asked to be retrained, he'd risked court martial, but he'd found out where his limits were and would not go beyond them. He knew what was right for him.

But then there was Connie. That was a betrayal. That wasn't right. He and Connie had been together.

Were they together though? When was the last time Dag had thought of her, really thought of her? Weeks? Months? What had he done instead, ranted at her, complained? He had driven her away.

His relationship with Connie had run its course. Roland and Connie were together not out of betrayal, but because they loved each other, they were right together. Douglas had always suspected it; his own actions had made it come true.

Connie had been unhappy with him, she would find happiness with Roland, they both would. Connie was right. Roland was right.

Roland was right.

What else was he right about?

He looked across at his engineer. Everyone in the squadron knew about the trauma he'd suffered, the sole survivor of his crew, bearing the scars of the disaster on his face and scalp. The scars no one could see, they were worse. They'd come out on this trip. He had kids too, and their mother was ill, Dag hadn't known that before. The truth was that he hadn't bothered to find out. It made sense now, the man had been distracted all yesterday and the reason was now clear. He needed to get back to his kids.

A good father. One who cared.

Not like Douglas's.

'Left, left, left - that's it.'

Taylor was going to be a dad. He hadn't known that either. In his own resentments, his selfishness, he hadn't bothered to find out. His crew hadn't mattered.

He'd taken risks, driven six other men's lives, five now, to the edge of losing everything.

But it didn't matter now, did it? They were there, at the target. They'd done it.

'Right, right.'

Roland was right.

He was.

Dropping their bombs on a target that was already destroyed would make no difference. It was morally wrong, it would do nothing but destroy his best friend's self-worth and beliefs. Roland cared, deeply. This could destroy him. What would it do to him and Connie?

LMF 99

27/1/44 1.57 am

R oland blinked away the tears. He held the bomb release button in his hand. The target was seconds
away, looming large through his bombsights.

Then it was gone. He felt C-Charlie bank steeply.

'Dag, I haven't -' he said.

'Roland, close the bomb bay doors,' Dag's voice was calm
over the intercom. 'Crew, listen up. This is what we're going to
do.'

Malcolm Havard

557 Squadron, Royal Air Force

Court of Inquiry Report

28/1/1944

Present: Acting W/C Harvey, S/L Mitchell, Captain A. Harper (panel)

Also Present: *Corporal Henson (minutes)*

1. This is the report of the Board of Inquiry into the conduct of the crew of H/P Halifax W1263, call sign C-Charlie, during the raid on ESSEN on the night of 26/27 January 1944.

2. On return, it became apparent that the crew had failed to bomb the target.

3. During debriefing, it further became apparent that the bombs had been deliberately expended on open countryside away from populated areas even though bombing of the target was possible.

4. On receipt of this information, a disciplinary board was assembled.

5. The board met on the afternoon of 27th January 1944 and heard testimony from the crew and received witness statements from other members of the squadron.

6. The following facts were established.

7. The squadron was informed by Bomber Command Headquarters by telex at 6.33 am on 26/1/44 that all available squadron aircraft were to be readied for a raid on military targets in ESSEN that night.

8. Details of the targets, timings, the squadron's place in the bomber stream, target marking and meteorological information were also distributed by bomber command.

9. (Acting) W/C HARVEY determined that eighteen (18) of the squadron's aircraft were serviceable and available for operations that night.

10. Accordingly, W/C HARVEY and Captain HARPER, the squadron adjutant, rostered eighteen of the duty crews for the operation.

11. The crew lists were posted on the relevant noticeboards.

12. Shortly after this had been done, W/C HARVEY was approached by Sergeant Pilot ATKINSON-GRIEVE who asked to fly on the night's raid in order to complete his tour of operations.

13. Sergeant ATKINSON-GRIEVE is an experienced pilot who had completed 29 missions prior to the raid on ESSEN.

14. He was not, at that time, attached to a regular crew, instead acting as a reserve pilot for the squadron.

15. Sergeant ATKINSON-GRIEVE was informed that the squadron roster was complete but that an additional aircraft could be added to the roll if the pilot was able to assemble a crew from those not due to fly that night.

16. Whilst ATKINSON-GRIEVE was recruiting his crew, W/C HARVEY consulted with senior squadron officers and the senior Medical Officer as to the pilot's suitability to fly. No serious objections were raised.

17. F/L SAUNDERS was the first crew member recruited.

18. SAUNDERS is a navigator who had served in ATKINSON-GRIEVE's original crew. He had just returned to the squadron after recovering from a non-operational injury. Prior to his injury. SAUNDERS had completed 14 missions.

19. F/L SAUNDERS recruited both air gunners and the bomb aimer from the officers' mess during breakfast.

20. The remaining crew members were obtained from the Sergeants' mess at the same time.

21. The suggested crew rota were supplied to the squadron office by 1000 hours.

22. In the meantime, a spare H/P Halifax, serial number W1263, was allocated to Sergeant ATKINSON-GRIEVE.

23. W1263 is a Halifax MKII srs 1A, built by the Rootes group and supplied new to the squadron in April 1943. It had completed 57 missions and had a good serviceability record.

24. The crew of C-Charlie were, therefore, Pilot - Sergeant ATKINSON-GRIEVE (dob 2/3/1923, 29 missions), Navigator - F/L SAUNDERS (dob 5/5/1922, 14 missions), Engineer - Sergeant HARRISON (dob 21/11/1907, 20 missions), Bomb aimer - P/O HOWARD (dob 17/7/1919, 5 missions), Radio operator - Sergeant HILEY (dob 22/12/1925, 0 missions), Mid-upper Gunner - F/L PASCOE (dob 3/5/1922, 12 missions) and, Rear Gunner - F/L TAYLOR (dob 1/8/1920, 12 missions)

25. Although this crew had never flown together prior to the night of 26/27 January 1944, members of the crew had served together, including, as noted the pilot and navigator, and also the two gunners.

26. With the exception of Sergeant HILEY, who had recently joined the squadron from a HCU, all had considerable operational experience.

27. All of the crew volunteered to fly on the mission.

28. The crew attended the general briefings as normal prior to the raid.

29. All of the specialist departmental briefings took place in the morning prior to the raid. The respective crew specialists attended their briefings.

30. The aircraft was checked over by the crew on the morning of the 26th and no problems were found.

31. The pilot and engineer carried out their inspection of the aircraft later than would normally have occurred but it is not believed that this had any impact on the preparation of the aircraft.

32. All the crews assigned to the raid, including that of C-Charlie, rested during the afternoon of 26th January.

33. The final target briefing went ahead as normal at 1630 hours. No specific issues with the target or its defences were identified.

33. The crews were briefed on the squadron's take-off time and their individual places in the overall bombing stream.

34. The first take-off was to be at 2005 with the last aircraft away at 2110.

35. As C-Charlie was a late addition to the squadron roll it was allocated the final take-off slot.

36. On completion of the briefing, an evening meal for the crews was served as normal in both the officers' and sergeants' messes.

37. The crews then dispersed to their aircraft. As embarkation took place, it was discovered that C-Charlie had developed a minor technical fault.

38. The aircraft was returned to a hangar for this to be resolved.

39. The aircraft's departure was delayed.

40. Despite the delay caused by the technical issue, the crew were happy to fly on the mission.

41. C-Charlie took off at around 2200 and climbed out over the

North Sea following the rest of the bomber stream.

42. C-Charlie climbed to its allocated altitude and followed the same route as the other bombers in the stream.

43. The initial part of the flight up to and including the first turn was reported as being perfectly normal.

44. The navigation log shows that the crew then made an unscheduled and unsanctioned course change that took C-Charlie on a more direct route over occupied Holland.

45. Light flak was encountered as the aircraft crossed the enemy coast.

46. The unsanctioned course coincided with an unofficial but widely used escape course for returning crews.

47. As a result, C-Charlie had to descend to avoid a collision with another, unknown aircraft.

48. No damage occurred in this incident and the crew pressed on.

49. Following the loss of altitude, C-Charlie attempted to climb back up to its assigned bombing height.

50. Some nightfighter activity was noted over the Dutch/German border.

51. C-Charlie took successful evasive action to avoid a nightfighter attack.

52. During the evasive manoeuvres, one of the engines developed a technical problem.

53. At some point, during the confusion of the fighter attack, the bomb aimer, p/o HOWARD, appears to have bailed out.

54. The remaining crew continued towards the target.

55. Other minor technical problems with the aircraft were encountered.

56. The aircraft was briefly caught in searchlights and suffered slight flak damage.

57. The technical problems and damage did not materially affect the functioning of the aircraft.

58. The bomb run commenced slightly before 0200 with F/L SAUNDERS acting as the bomb aimer.

59. The pilot then took the decision to abort the bomb run and instructed f/l SAUNDERS to jettison the bombs on open ground away from any built up areas.

60. The aircraft then turned for home, arriving at the airfield at

0441 hours.

61. In the debrief, Sergeant ATKINSON-GRIEVE told both the intelligence officer and the commanding officer that he had ordered that no attack should be made and that he took total responsibility for this.

62. This court of inquiry was then initiated.

FINDINGS

63. The court finds sergeant ATKINSON-GRIEVE guilty of dereliction of duty.

64. The sentence of the court is that he should be demoted to Aircraftman, dismissed from the squadron, removed from flight service and that his record should be amended to show that he has a lack or moral fibre.

65. All other crew members should return to normal duties.

66. The court of inquiry adjourned at 1635 hours on 27/1/44.

INVESTIGATION 2

12.25 am 6th February 1944

Murray looked again at the minutes of the court of inquiry and then at the crew debriefs taken immediately after they had landed.

There were differences.

Yes, generally they accorded but some details were missing. If you were being generous you could interpret that was as a result of the inquiry concentrating on the important facts. If you weren't then the omissions looked like deliberate obfuscation.

Nowhere in the official report was it mentioned that Pascoe had shot down a nightfighter in the midst of what was clearly a sustained attack - two separate attacks in fact. The vague mentions of 'technical problems' glossed over a total engine failure and a non-operational rear turret, both surely grounds for C-Charlie turning back?

Then there was Saunders, not only had he stood in for the bomb aimer, at one point he seemed to have acted as the engineer too. Where had Harrison been? The crew debrief was silent on that, in fact they had refused to answer direct questions about him.

So, there were things missing from the crew debriefs.

And other gaps, significantly about what had happened over the target. They had all said the same thing: 'We turned back. We jettisoned the bombs.'

There was no explanation of why.

But the biggest omission in the debriefs concerned the pilot. There wasn't one. The man who had been found LMF only appeared in the inquiry minutes. The condemned man had no voice.

Murray's thoughts were interrupted by a light but sharp rap on the door which was then pushed open.

It was Harvey.

'You done?' he said. 'Ready for lunch?'

'Erm...well...'

'Oh come on, you can't have doubts? It's pretty clear isn't it? Dag freely admitted what he'd done.'

'Dag?'

'Atkinson-Grieve. That's what everyone called him.'

Murray frowned. 'Called? Past tense?'

'Yes. He's left, been shipped out. Wanted to save him some face. Why?'

Murray looked down at the papers. 'I wanted a word with him.'

'Why?'

'Because there are no debrief notes for him, nothing that gives his point of view.'

Harvey shrugged. 'There's no debrief because he came straight to me and told me what he'd done.'

'So we've only got your...' Murray began, then thought better of it.

Even so, Harvey looked affronted. 'Are you saying I

made it up?' he demanded.

'No, of course not. I just -'

'He told me in no uncertain terms. He was proud of it. I can't see how you've got any doubts.'

Murray stared at the squadron leader for a few moments, then picked up Dag's personal file. 'The man had done 29 trips, nearly a full tour. By the sound of it he did 99% of his 30th, driving the crew on through some serious technical problems -'

'What serious problems?'

'Well, the crew debriefs -'

'Crews exaggerate to make what they did sound better. Everyone knows that.' He held up his hands as if to ward off an expected protest from Murray. 'I'm not saying deliberately, but anyone who's done a trip knows that you come back high as a kite from the thrill of it. Chaps get carried away, you need to take what they say with a pinch of salt.'

The barb was clear. 'Anyone who's done a trip.' Murray tried not to rise to it.

Surely, then, the pilot was in the same boat,' he said. 'Why not take what he said with a pinch of salt too?'

'Don't you dare twist my words like that!' Harvey yelled. 'That's beyond the pale. If you want the truth, this would have been an open and shut case except for one thing: Dag's father. Dag's a love child, the bastard son of a General who had a fling with the maid. Everyone knows it, and that's why Dag's got such an almighty chip on his shoulder. The old man's now a staff officer, he keeps a weather eye on his boy, and he needs to because Dag is trouble, always has been. He's why you're here, even if you don't know it. He's pulled strings and you're at the end of the cord.'

Harvey took a deep breath. It was obvious he was trying to recover his temper. He shook his head, gave a little rueful smile and raised his eyebrows to the heavens. 'I'm sorry,

Murray. The bloody man still manages to wind me up even after he's gone. I didn't mean to blow my top, this isn't your fault, you're only doing what you've been told to. What else can I do to help?'

'Could I speak to Saunders?' Murray said.

'Ah, no. I'm afraid he's off on a refresher course.'

'The rear gunner, Taylor?'

'On compassionate leave. Wife's had a baby.'

'Harrison?'

'On his way to Australia. His wife's really sick.'

Murray stared at the squadron leader. 'Are any of the crew on the base?'

'No. Pascoe's gone to be a gunnery instructor and Hiley's on sick leave.' Harvey smiled. 'You've not had the best of luck, have you?'

'No, I haven't.' Murray looked down at the debriefs again. 'Wait. Hiley was injured? Surely that confirms the reports, doesn't it?'

'Not really. He's a sprog, first mission. There are plenty of things to trip over on ops, and the lad's'll say anything to cover themselves.' Harvey gave a condescending smile. 'Anyone who'd flown on ops would know that. Now, lunch?'

Murray had one last try. 'What about the machine? Can I give it a look over?'

'Sorry, been scrapped. We're getting the new Hercules powered crates, so we're phasing out the old ones. C-Charlie was the oldest we had, so it was first to go.' He smiled. 'Come on, let's go and eat. I don't know about you but I'm starving.'

Accepting defeat, Murray got to his feet.

LMF 100

27/1/44 4.42 am

Harvey watched C-Charlie taxi up to its stand by the hangar.

It was the fifteenth aircraft back and, given the time, would be the last. Four missing, that was about par for the course. He thought it had been five but, of course, like a bad penny, Dag always turned up.

But at least he'd be rid of him now. His tour was done. He'd be someone else's problem now.

He decided he should show some class. Congratulate the sod. Thanks and goodbye.

As he walked across, he noticed something odd. There were only six of them by the aircraft. Where was the other crew member? Dead? No, they hadn't called for an ambulance. So, where was he? And what was that WAAF officer doing hugging Saunders? When had that started? It wouldn't do, he'd get it nipped that in the bud.

By the time he reached the crew, Saunders had let go of the WAAF and was stood in earnest conversation with Dag. He looked unhappy, he was shaking his head. What had Dag done to upset him this time?

'No, Dag, you can't,' Harvey heard Saunders say.

'I can,' said Dag. 'Stick to the story. All of you.'

Harvey walked right up to them. Saunders and the rest saluted. Dag didn't.

'What story?' said Harvey. 'Come on, out with it. What story?'

'We...' began Saunders.

'The only story is the truth,' said Dag. 'That we bombed Germany.'

'Well good,'

'But we didn't bomb the target.'

'Why not? Didn't you find it?'

'Oh we found it all right, but I decided not to bomb it.'

'You...what?'

'You heard.'

'Why?'

'Because I...' began Saunders.

'Because it wasn't necessary. And it wasn't right,' said Dag. 'Off you go, now lads, I want a word in private with the CO. Get some coffee and do the debrief. I'll be along in a minute.' The crew started to walk away. 'Oh Lads,' added Dag. 'Thank you, for all you did tonight. And remember what I said.'

There were weary nods. Only Saunders briefly looked like hesitating but, eventually, he too joined the rest.

Harvey watched them go before turning on the pilot again. 'Right, what's this nonsense? What the hell do you mean, it wasn't necessary?'

But, to Harvey's surprise - and anger - Dag just smiled and started to walk away. 'Read it in the debrief,' he said. 'I'm done.'

Harvey grabbed Dag's arm and jerked him around. 'You cheeky bastard, don't you turn your back on me. Answer me, here, now.'

Dag pulled himself free.

'Right, I'll answer you, I'll bloody well tell you. We didn't bomb the town because it was already destroyed. Our bombs would have done nothing but add a bit more misery and kill a few more civilians. What would have been the point?'

'The point? The point?' Harvey shouted. 'The point is that's what we do, what we train you and your crew to do, it's why we give you kit like this.' He pointed at C-Charlie.

'Oh yeah, kit like this!' Dag pointed too. 'A bloody deathtrap, it's falling apart. It's got clapped out engines and busted hydraulics. You knew that yet you sent us out in it, me and the rest of the crew. And that crew, look at them. Misfits, expendables, you didn't care if we didn't come back, did you? You wouldn't have shed any tears, would you? Well, I'm sorry, I've done my job, I've done my tour, and I've brought your bloody misfits back. At least I'm out of here now.'

He turned away again.

'Damned well stand still!' Harvey screamed. 'I'm not finished with you yet. I'm your bloody CO.'

Dag stopped but didn't turn around.

'And don't I bloody know it,' he said. 'Technically, you *were* my CO, but, I said, I'm done.'

'You're not done! Not until I say you are! You've not finished your tour.'

'I have. I bombed Germany. A field, admittedly, not a town but it was probably more useful. Who knows, we may have killed a few cows.'

This time he did walk off and no amount of shouting by Harvey brought him back.

INVESTIGATION

3

2.20 pm 6th February 1944

'Right then, Murray, if you're all done, we'd better get you to the station.' Harvey stared at his visitor. 'You are done, aren't you?' he added, in a tone that brooked no arguments.

'Yes, of course,' Murray replied, in no doubt that he was being railroaded into a decision and hurried off the airfield.

'Feel free to wait in my office whilst we get your car organised.'

'Actually, if you don't mind, I'd like to get a breath of air and stretch my legs before being cooped up on the train for God knows how long.'

'Of course.' Harvey held out his hand, smiling. 'Good to have met you, Murray.'

With some reluctance, Murray shook it.

Outside, he had no plans as to where he would he go, he just knew that he wanted to be away from people for a while. People lied - no, perhaps lied was too strong a word, they dissembled, produced their own version of events. But did he even know that for certain? No, he didn't. It was convenient for the squadron's position that Atkinson-Grieve's medical records had been 'sent on' and were unavailable. He couldn't even view the physical evidence of the aircraft. Yes, he had the crew's debriefs but they had been dismissed as 'exaggerated' and he had nothing to corroborate them.

He'd reached a dead end. His trip had been a waste of time. A pilot who had survived 29 difficult and dangerous missions, who had twice been recommended for decorations, who had flown a 30th mission whilst almost certainly suffering with his nerves if not some other neurological problems, had been shamed, demoted and branded as LMF.

It just didn't seem right.

But what could he do about it?

He found he was by one of the giant hangars. Inside the mechanics were working on the squadron's Halifaxes. Two of them looked different from the rest, their paintwork and markings were crisp and fresh, and the four engines were snub-nosed and bulkier than the close-cowled Merlins of the other, more war weary machines. Murray realised that these must be the new MkIIIs, the much improved latest Halifaxes.

Would they have made a difference for the crew of C-Charlie? He'd never know.

He was getting cold. He turned to return to the admin block but then something caught his eye. The tip of a wing, projecting from behind the hangar, only visible from this position.

Although it had started raining, he was curious. The aircraft had been hidden from view, why? There was only one way to find out.

He was already chilled from the weather but the cold within him deepened when he got close to the machine. All the markings - the squadron codes and the serial numbers - had been roughly painted out, the paint still wet in places suggesting it had been done that morning, since Murray had arrived in fact. He was sure which aircraft this was though; it had to be C-Charlie.

There was so much that accorded with the briefing reports for it not to be. The port outer's propeller was feathered, the blades edge on to the airstream. The cowling of the engine and the wing were smoke blackened and streaked with oil. Walking around to the back of the aircraft he reached the rear turret. The guns had been removed but there were words scrawled in white paint nearby on the fuselage: 'U/S - do not salvage'.

He completed a full circuit of the machine. Myriad holes pockmarked the metal skin, not big but clear signs that it had been struck several times by flak and bullets. The perspex on both turrets were cracked. A large chunk of the windscreen and part of the cockpit top was missing.

This aircraft had, literally, been in the wars. The truth about what had really happened was there, written in its scars.

But what could he do? He had no camera, he couldn't take the machine with him. Yes, he could take notes but what weight would they have? Harvey would deny that this was C-Charlie.

The truth was that Atkinson-Grieve - Dag - had let this happen. He'd sat quietly through the court of inquiry, he'd not defended himself. It was like he wanted the result, wanted to hurt himself.

Or hurt his father by letting it happen?

Who knew? Murray suddenly felt weary, what was the point of him being here, what was the point of all of this? Pounding towns and cities to oblivion, paying lip service to hitting military targets when everyone knew it was the civilians themselves who were the targets. Dag had been right, he probably had done more to win the war by killing livestock and depriving the German army of a few hundred pounds of meat than bombing an already wrecked town.

That was Dag's achievement. That and getting most of his crew there and back in this shed of an aircraft. That was amazing but, to the RAF, that was clearly not enough.

He turned and walked away from the aircraft. It was pointless. There was nothing he could do about the decision, even though it was patently obvious that it was wrong. He didn't have the evidence to overturn it.

Pointless, the whole thing, a waste of time, everything, his mission, Dag's, the crew of C-Charlie, probably the whole bloody bombing campaign.

It was time he got out of there.

EPILOGUE

4.15 pm 3rd March 1944

He stood on the platform as the train hissed, clanked and pulled away in a cloud of steam. He waited until it had gone then closed his eyes and took a long in-breath through his nose.

The scents were unmistakable: heat, eucalyptus tinged with dust. The scent of home.

He had travelled a long way, in so many senses. He still had a few miles to go to really be home but there was somewhere he needed to go first. Not that he wanted to, but he knew he had to.

He opened his eyes, shouldered his kit bag and set off.

Ten minutes or so later he was there. Again, he stood quietly at first staring straight ahead, his eyes on the distant horizon, looking but not seeing. His vision blurred, as it had over Germany six weeks before but for very different reasons.

At last, he forced himself to look down.

He saw the mound of red earth, the soil familiar in its blocky, stubborn dryness. At the end of the mound was a new, redwood cross.

It was a devastating, almost overwhelming sight, even though it was exactly as he'd pictured it. The thing was that this was final confirmation of reality, of what had, until now, been a distant and unreal nightmare, one that he could hope to wake up from.

But he was already awake. It was real, he always knew that. This was it now, this was his here, his now and his future. His whole reason for living now was clear and starkly laid out.

He was scared. But he could do it. He had to.

'G'day Mags, old girl,' said Burt. 'I'm home. I'll look after the kids. No worries.'

A MESSAGE FROM THE AUTHOR

Hi, I really hope you enjoyed LMF. Even if you didn't I do have a request.

I'm an independent author, I don't have a publishing company behind me with a massive marketing budget, promoting my books is not easy.

One thing that does help is a review. Please could you spare a few minutes to review this book on Amazon or Goodreads? Good or bad, I don't mind, I would much prefer an honest review than no review at all. It helps spread the word and it gives me some feedback too.

It would be much appreciated if you could do this.

Thanks in advance.

Malcolm Havard
Cheshire, UK, 2019

Printed in Great Britain
by Amazon

57377857R00170